Cracked Reflection

Zayn Jamshaid

Published by Zayn, 2024.

CRACKED REFLECTION

First edition. October 15, 2024.

ISBN: 979-8227614636

Written by Zayn Jamshaid.

Table of Contents

0 - The Vanishing 1

1 - Skeptic 5

2 - Sarah Lawson 11

3 - Doubt & the Paranormal 18

4 - The Wondersun Family 25

5 - Sins of Our Fathers 34

6 - Reflection 42

7 - The Weight Of Loss 48

8 - Rainy Reunion 53

9 - Haunted Mirrors & Gregg...................................... 60

10 - Broken Bridges 71

11 - Into the Abyss... 76

12 - Raven Wondersun 91

13 - Endings & Beginnings... 98

Author's Note 109

To my Baba,Thank you for teaching me not only the importance of standing by family and friends but also the path to being closer to Allah. Through your faith and guidance, I learned the beauty of relying on Him in all things. Your lessons in companionship, brotherhood, and faith live on in my heart. I hope that every good I do reflects what you taught me. May Allah grant you Jannat ul Firdous and eternal peace. I miss you, but your love, wisdom, and faith continue to guide me. I love you.

0 - The Vanishing

Fears and secrets have a way of surfacing, no matter how deeply they're buried—they always find a way back into the light. Try as you might to hide them, they linger in the shadows, waiting for the moment when your guard is down, when you're most vulnerable. And when they finally emerge, there's no telling what they'll destroy in their wake.

The air was thick with anticipation as Jessica and her two friends entered the Crestfall Museum. As they moved deeper into the museum, the oppressive darkness seemed to close in on them, amplifying every whisper and footstep. The air grew colder, and an unsettling silence replaced the usual hum of the town outside. Despite their bravado, a palpable tension hung among the group, fueled by the legends surrounding the museum's most infamous exhibit: the mirror.

"Why are we doing this right now? At 2 a.m.?" Amy muttered, her phone's flashlight casting an uneasy glow.

"Because it's more fun," Danny replied, his attempt at nonchalance barely masking his own unease. "Right, Jess?"

Jessica forced a laugh. "Totally. It's just a story, anyway."

As they navigated through the museum, the dim light from their phones cast eerie shadows on the ancient artifacts. Amy walked behind Danny and Jessica, every step filled with nerve and fear. Amy stopped and noticed a strange yet beautiful artifact. "Amy! Stay close!" Jessica exclaimed as Amy rushed back to her side. As Amy returned, she noticed something; Danny was nowhere to be found.

"Danny!" Amy silently yelled out. "Don't be a dickhead! Where are you?!"

As Jessica and Amy began trying to look for Danny, they heard rumbling coming from a window.

"Uh, Amy?" Jessica asked, her heart starting to race.

"No, Jess, that isn't me," Amy replied as she walked toward the window. She noticed it was shaking, and as she slowly opened it, her hands trembled. As she popped her head outside...

"Boo!" Danny said, popping his head out. Amy screamed and backed away.

"Haha!" Danny laughed.

"You fucking asshole!" Amy said, trying to calm herself down. "After this, I'm not fucking hanging with you anymore."

Danny started laughing again. "You should have seen the look on your face." Jessica looked to her right and noticed a small room. "Hey guys, check this out."

Finally, they found themselves in a small, dusty room at the back of the building. There, dominating the back wall, stood the mirror. Its ornate frame was covered in intricate carvings, and the surface gleamed darkly despite the dim lighting.

"That's it," Danny said, his voice barely a whisper.

They formed a semicircle around the mirror, none daring to step closer. The legends claimed those who looked into it would see their deepest fears, their darkest secrets. Jessica's heart pounded in her chest. Her hands trembled as she reached out to touch the dusty edge of the mirror, her breath coming in short, uneven bursts. Her heart raced with each creak of the floor, a stark contrast to Danny's forced bravado and Amy's palpable fear. Jessica's mind flashed back to the fateful day—her mother's eyes filled with sudden terror, the screech of tires, and the bone-jarring impact. The memory surfaced with a haunting clarity, as if the mirror was already whispering her guilt.

"Who's going first?" Danny asked, trying to sound casual but failing miserably.

"I'll do it," Jessica said, stepping forward. Determination surged through her; she wouldn't let fear control her.

She stood before the mirror, her reflection staring back. For a moment, nothing happened. She turned to her friends with a smirk. "See? Just a stor—"

A whisper cut through the air. "Jessicaaaa."

She froze, the sound chilling her to the bone. Turning back, she saw her mother's ghostly face in the mirror, eyes filled with cold accusation.

"Mom?" Jessica's voice cracked, terror flooding her as memories overwhelmed her.

"It's your fault I died," the reflection said, its voice piercing through her.

"No," Jessica whimpered, tears spilling down her cheeks. The room trembled, objects rattling.

"If you weren't distracting me that day, I'd be alive.," the reflection continued, its tone harsh and unforgiving.

Jessica started shaking, her head throbbing. "Jessica!" Amy yelled as Danny held her back. The reflection spoke once again, "It's all because of you."

Jessica fell to her knees, sobbing. "I'm sorry, Mom. I'm so sorry."

Her friends watched in horror, frozen. The reflection's eyes glowed a menacing red, and its lips curved into a sinister smile. "Don't worry, I forgive you," it sneered.

The mirror's surface rippled like liquid mercury as a cold, spectral hand emerged, its fingers clawing at the air. Jessica's scream was swallowed by the dark, as the hand wrapped around her wrist, pulling her with a force she couldn't resist. The glass seemed to stretch and distort, swallowing her whole with a chilling, echoing gasp.

"Jessica!" Danny screamed, but it was too late. Her cries echoed as Jessica vanished, the mirror returning to its smooth, unbroken state.

Panic erupted. Danny was the first to bolt, followed closely by Amy, their terror-filled screams echoing through the empty halls. The legends were no longer just stories; they were real, and Crestfall's legend had claimed another victim.

1 - Skeptic

"**E**veryone, stay back!" An officer said as he signed for the press to back off of the crime scene. A car pulled along the curb of the museum, a woman and a man got out of the vehicle and walked to the front of the entrance. "Lawson, McAlaney, we got a crazy one today." The officer said as he looked at the two.

"You're telling me. a haunted mirror? Fuckin' nuts." Detective Sarah Lawson said as she and Officer Gregg McAlaney entered the museum. The air was thick with the scent of aged wood and dust, mingling with a faint mustiness that clung to the back of their throats. The floorboards creaked ominously underfoot, echoing through the dimly lit halls. Her partner, Officer Gregg McAlaney, followed closely, his eyes scanning the dimly lit room with an intensity she found both amusing and slightly unnerving.

"You really think she got sucked into a mirror?" Sarah asked, her voice tinged with skepticism as they approached the scene.

Gregg shrugged. "I try to be open minded about these type of stories."

"Stories," Sarah replied, her tone dismissive. "Urban legends to scare kids. Nothing more."

Sarah didn't believe in the supernatural, she hated stories and legends; She hated what she couldn't explain even more. They approached the infamous mirror, its ornate frame looming ominously. The room felt colder, Sarah shivered.

Gregg examined the floor closely, noting the fine layer of dust disturbed only by the recent chaos. Small scratches and grooves in the dust hinted at a struggle, while a closer inspection revealed smudged fingerprints near the mirror's base. It looked like no one had stepped in the room for weeks. "Look at these marks. Something happened here." Gregg stated.

"Or someone staged it," Sarah countered, crossing her arms. "Let's not jump to conclusions."

Gregg went over and stood in front of the mirror, he noticed how the air felt colder and congested in front of the mirror. He ignored it.

As they walked through the museum, Sarah felt a sudden chill, a breeze that shouldn't be there in the closed building. She shrugged it off, but the hairs on the back of her neck stood on end. Nevertheless, there was no sign of forced entry and no sign where Jessica could have been taken.

Sarah sighed, closing her notebook. "We're not finding anything here. Let's visit Jessica's family. Maybe they can give us some insight," she suggested, glancing at Gregg who nodded in agreement.

After some digging, they found her address and decided to visit Jessica's family.

As they arrived in the neighborhood of Jessica's house, Sarah stared out the car window, the town's streets passing by in a blur. Her mind raced with thoughts of the case, the unsettling atmosphere of the museum, and the haunted mirror's legend. Despite her disbelief, something about this case gnawed at her. "There's no way this is real, right?" she thought, glancing at Gregg, who seemed equally lost in thought.

Sarah and Gregg walked up along the front steps and proceeded to knock on the door. An old and weary-looking woman answered, her eyes red from crying.

"I'm Detective Lawson, and this is Officer McAlaney. We'd like to ask you some questions about Jessica."

The woman nodded, letting them in. The house was a small, cozy space, filled with memories of happier times. Framed photos covered the walls, each telling a story of love and loss. An old clock ticked loudly in the quiet room, its rhythmic sound underscoring the heaviness of the moment. The grandmother's hands shook slightly as she gestured to a photo of Jessica and her mother, her eyes filling with fresh tears. The grandmother's hands trembled in grief as she held the frame, "Jessica mentioned her mother's accident often," the woman said as even more tears rolled down from her eyes, her voice trembling as she noticed Sarah looking at the photos. She clutched the edge of her sweater, her knuckles white. "She always blamed herself."

"What happened to her mother? Ms. Smith?" Sarah said as Gregg picked up the photo, the woman looked down. "My daughter died in a car crash a couple of years back." She said as more tears began to build, "My granddaughter always thought that it was her fault," she said, her voice breaking into a whisper.

She wiped her eyes with a trembling hand, the grief in her gaze piercing through Sarah's skepticism. "She would cry for hours, saying she should have been less troublesome."

The woman got up holding the picture frame in her hands, "Blaming yourself for your past. It... it only binds you to what you cannot change," she said, her voice cracking as tears welled up. She looked down at the photo, her fingers trembling. "I've made mistakes with my daughter and I've moved on from it, but the idea of losing Jessica... she's the only family I have left," she continued, her voice breaking into sobs.

Jessica and Gregg looked at each other in realizing the gravity of the situation and the fact that they needed to find Jessica fast. "Thank you, ma'am. Rest assured, we're working hard to find your granddaughter." Gregg said as he tried comforting the woman.

Sarah and Gregg walked out of the house, "Thank you." Sarah exclaimed as she shut the front door. Sarah and Gregg walked down the steps, "Detective, why don't we ask the kid's friends about what happened again." He said scratching his head, Gregg scratched his head, looking genuinely puzzled. "Cause I honestly don't know what to do from here," he admitted.

Sarah gave him a reassuring pat on the shoulder. "We'll figure it out, Gregg. We always do," she said, a hint of a smile playing at her lips. Their partnership, though strained at times, had always been built on trust and mutual respect.

As they walked back to the car, Sarah's thoughts drifted to her own past. She had lost her father in an accident years ago, and the guilt still haunted her. She never talked about it, not even to Gregg, but the pain was always there. "Maybe that's why this case is getting to me," she thought, the weight of her own unresolved grief pressing down on her.

Sarah looked back at the house. She couldn't help but see a reflection of her own life in Jessica's story— the mistakes, the guilt. Memories of her own unresolved past tugged at her, but she shook herself out of it. "Yeah, I'm still having trouble believing that there's a haunted mirror in Crestfall," she said, though doubt gnawed at her.

Later, back at the station, Sarah sat across from Jessica's friends, their faces pale and anxious. "Tell me what happened that night again, " she said.

They recounted the story, their voices trembling as they described the mirror and Jessica's disappearance. Sarah listened carefully, noting the consistency in their accounts, despite the unbelievable nature of their claims.

"You don't believe us, do you?" Amy asked, frustration edging her voice.

"I'm here to find the truth," Sarah replied, maintaining her composure. "But I need facts, not a ghost story."

"It's not a story anymore!" Danny exclaimed as his fist struck the desk, "Jessica stood in the mirror, we saw her mom and then it pulled her in! Jessica is gone and you guys aren't doing anything about it!" Danny yelled as tears began to well up in his eyes.

Gregg calmed Danny down, "Look kid, we're doing everything we can." He said as he began escorting Danny and Amy out. "But, you gotta understand how crazy your guys' stories sound."

"Fuck this." Amy yelled. As Danny and Amy walked away, Amy's jaw clenched with determination. "If they won't do anything, *we* will," she muttered to Danny, fire burning in her eyes. Danny nodded as he cleaned the tears in his eyes, his face set with resolve.

As they left the station, Gregg turned to her. "You're really not buying any of this, are you?"

"No.." Sarah said, her mind racing with possibilities. "I- I don't know."

Gregg pulled out his phone, checking the time. "We should grab a coffee before heading back to the station," he suggested, trying to lighten the mood. Sarah nodded, grateful for his attempt to keep things normal. "You and your coffee," she teased, a small smile breaking through her serious demeanor. "Hey, it's my one vice," Gregg replied with a grin, his easygoing nature a stark contrast to Sarah's intensity.

They arrived back at the station and Sarah dove into her chair, she looked up at Gregg who was drinking an extra large coffee, "You need to lay off the coffee, dude."

Gregg looked back up at Sarah, "Says the woman who drinks her weight in tea." He said with a smirk. Sarah chuckled, "Touche." She said. Sarah looked up at the ceiling, this case was strange but the investigation was far from over, and as skeptical as she was, Sarah felt like she owed it to Jessica's grandmother and Jessica's friends to uncover the truth behind her disappearance and Crestfall's supposed haunted mirror.

2 - Sarah Lawson

"Sarah! Jenny!" Teena called from the kitchen, "Dinner's ready!"

"Coming!" the sisters shouted back in unison. Sarah bounded down the stairs, Jenny close on her heels. Sarah grabbed her plate and stood in line, a smirk on her face as she waited for their mother to serve the food.

"Hey! Why do you get food first?" Jenny protested, trying to push her way to the front.

"Because I'm older," Sarah declared, her smirk widening.

Jenny rolled her eyes. "Relax, sis, you're only two years older than me." She gave Sarah a playful shove, but Sarah held her ground.

"I'm 17," Sarah retorted, "I'm basically almost an adult."

Their father, Tom, walked into the kitchen, his clothes smeared with grease from working on his car. "Keyword: almost," he said with a chuckle.

Teena joined in, her laughter lightening the room. "If it's any consolation, you both are idiots," she teased as she placed food onto Sarah's plate first.

As Jenny stepped up for her food, she grabbed a fork and joked, "This is abuse. I'm calling CPS."

Teena looked up at Jenny, a mischievous glint in her eye. "Ha! Call 'em to take both yer' asses away."

Jenny smiled, grabbing her plate. Teena then turned to Tom. "Tom, are you hungry?" she asked as he sat down at the table.

"Yes, ma'am," he said, placing a napkin on his lap. "Load it up, please."

Teena smiled warmly at her husband. Tom then remembered something. "Hey, Sarah? Could you please get my phone from the garage? It's on the stool beside the car."

Sarah sprang up from her chair. "Jen, don't take anything from my plate!" she warned as she darted towards the garage.

In the dimly lit garage, the air was thick with the smell of motor oil and metal. A lamp by the desk flickering. Sarah navigated around her father's damaged red car, her eyes scanning for the stool. She found it, the phone resting precariously on top. As she bent down to grab it, she noticed something- something spreading like a dark and sinister stain beneath the car. There was a large pool of black oil spreading beneath the car. A shiver ran down her spine, but she brushed it off, assuming her dad was working on something.

Sarah hurried back into the kitchen, her dad's phone in hand. "Here, Father," she said, adopting a mock formal tone.

Tom took the phone, playing along. "Thank you, Daughter."

The family settled into their meal. Jenny, unable to resist, began making faces at Sarah. Annoyed, Sarah turned to their mother. "Mom, tell Jenny to stop," she complained, giving Jenny a light punch on the arm.

"Ow!" Jenny yelped, rubbing her arm.

Teena's voice rose. "Both of you, knock it off. We're eating."

Tom intervened, his tone firm but kind. "Cool it, both of you. You're sisters; you've got to watch out for each other. Now, apologize." He glanced between Sarah and Jenny, waiting for their response.

Sarah and Jenny rolled their eyes simultaneously. "Sorry, Sarah," Jenny mumbled first.

Sarah smirked. "I ain't," she said, unable to contain her laughter.

Teena and Tom exchanged exasperated glances, silently communicating their shared annoyance with the sibling banter. "Unbelievable," Tom muttered, finishing his meal and standing up. "Anyway, I'm almost done with the car. I'll be out in a minute."

Sarah and Jenny cleared their plates, placing them in the sink as Teena started washing dishes. Sarah then climbed the stairs to her room. Before she dove into her bed, Sarah lingered by her door, ready to shout goodnight to her parents and sister. But just as she opened her mouth, a sharp pain shot through her head. "Ow!" she exclaimed, holding her temple.

Shaking off the pain, Sarah headed downstairs to say goodnight. But before she could, Teena's scream pierced the air. "TOM!"

Sarah bolted down the stairs, Jenny close behind. The garage door was open, and what Sarah saw would haunt her forever—her father was engulfed in flames. Teena frantically threw water on him, but the fire had already done its damage. Tom's body was charred and unrecognizable.

Jenny's sobs filled the room as she clung to her mother. Teena, tears streaming down her face, checked Tom's pulse, her voice breaking. "TOM! STAY WITH ME!" she screamed, attempting CPR.

Sarah stood frozen, her mind racing. Sarah then felt a pang in her heart, the realization hitting her. The oil, it wasn't on purpose; the car was leaking, and she hadn't told her dad. Guilt and horror washed over her. She fell to her knees, sobbing uncontrollably. Suddenly, her head throbbed again, with the smell of burning oil lingering in her nostrils.

A voice broke through the haze. "Detective? Detective?" A voice echoed in her mind.

"Detective!" The voice repeated more urgently.

Sarah jolted awake from her dream, her heart pounding. "WHAT?!" she gasped, disoriented, her mind trying to shake off the vivid image of her father engulfed in flames. Sarah gave herself a minute to catch her breath before looking up to her partner, Gregg. "Sorry, Gregg, bad dream," she said, clearing the books on the table.

Gregg put a stack of newspapers on the desk in Detective Lawson's office. "Don't worry. I've had those before too."

Sarah spaced the newspapers out. "What are these?" she asked, curious.

Gregg pointed to one of the newspapers. "Over the last seven decades, almost 12 people have supposedly been taken by this 'haunted mirror.'" He began reading from one of the articles, "'Local historian Susan Greendale reported missing. Witnesses say she was last seen near the antique mirror.'"

"I swear, this town is fuckin' crazy," Sarah said, picking up one of the newspapers. "Let's go back to the museum. I'll show you it's not haunted. We'll talk to the owner too."

Sarah and Gregg gathered their belongings and headed out. As Sarah and Gregg exited the office, they were stopped by Police Captain Wilson, "You two, you guys still on the Jessica Smith case?" he said. Sarah turned to the captain, "Yes sir, this case is strange but we'll work through it."

The captain gave an exasperated sigh, "Look, your top priority is to find Jessica Smith. Please don't get caught up in the whole urban legend." he said looking concerned.

Sarah and Gregg quickly looked at each other then back at the captain, "O—Of course," Gregg stated.

Thirty minutes later, they arrived at the museum, the sun rising behind them. They entered and were greeted by the owner, Tyson Lackson.

"Officers! Back so soon?" Tyson exclaimed.

Gregg reassured him, "Don't worry, Mr. Lackson, we just want to see if we missed anything. We'll be out of your way in no time."

Gregg and Sarah proceeded to the room with the mirror. They both entered, the dark room, with shadow casting from the window, almost evoking the feeling of being watched. Sarah walked in front of the mirror, scrutinizing its ornate frame and reflective surface.

"Everyone says you're haunted," she mumbled, staring into the mirror. Nothing happened. "See?" she exclaimed to Gregg. "It's just a story."

Gregg felt a twinge of disappointment. "Honestly, part of me thought it might be true," he admitted, walking out of the room. Sarah followed closely behind. Just as she was about to leave the room, she heard a faint sound—like liquid pouring—coming from the mirror.

She turned back towards the mirror and, to her horror, saw a reflection that wasn't there before. It was a stool with a phone placed on it, surrounded by a pool of black oil.

Sarah's heart raced as the reflection of the oil-surrounded stool flickered in the mirror. Her pulse quickened, and she felt a cold sweat forming on her brow. She tried to rationalize what she saw but a nagging fear gnawed at the edges of her mind.

She then felt a chill down her spine, her mind trying to comprehend the sight before her.

A wave of nausea hit Sarah as she stared even closer at the reflection. Memories of her father's incident hit her like a dump truck. Her knees felt weak, and she gripped the edge of the table for support. "Fuck. It-it can't be..." she whispered, her voice barely audible. The guilt she had buried for years resurfaced, threatening to overwhelm her.

"Detective, you coming?" Gregg's voice broke through her thoughts. He had re-entered the room, looking concerned.

Sarah looked at Gregg, then back at the mirror. The disturbing reflection was gone. She took a deep breath and walked slowly towards Gregg.

"You okay?" Gregg asked, noticing her distress.

Sarah didn't reply, still distracted by the disturbing image she had just witnessed, trying to reconcile reality with what she just saw.

"Detective?" Gregg repeated.

"Huh? Yeah, I- I thought I saw something," Sarah said, trying to shake off the unease. She walked out, Gregg's eyebrow raised as he glanced back at the mirror and then at Sarah. He followed her closely.

As Sarah approached Tyson, she cleaned the sweat off of her forehead.

The two then approached Tyson Lackson. "Mr. Lackson, do you know anything about the mirror's history?" Sarah asked, still shaken by what she had seen.

"Do you really believe it's haunted? Come on, it's just a story!" Tyson exclaimed.

Sarah shrugged off his skepticism. "Just the history, please."

Tyson sighed. "I know nothing about it. I bought it off an auction house. The whole urban legend is good publicity." He paused. "There was a guy who tried to buy it off me, but I didn't sell it to him."

Sarah's curiosity piqued. "Did he give you an address or a business card?"

"A business card. I'll get it for you." Tyson began searching through his phone.

Gregg asked, "Did he give you his name?"

Tyson replied, "Yeah, If I recall... I think it's- Samuel Blackwood."

3 - Doubt & the Paranormal

Sarah and Gregg walked up the gravel path to Samuel Blackwood's Victorian-style house. The evening was settling in, casting long shadows as the sun dipped below the horizon. The house loomed ahead, its tall, wrought-iron fence and overgrown hedges giving it an air of neglect that was both eerie and foreboding.

Sarah's steps were deliberate, though her mind was preoccupied. Gregg noticed the change in her demeanor—the skepticism that had always marked her approach to this case seemed to have shifted. "You're more interested in this mirror than you've let on," he remarked, his tone both curious and teasing.

Sarah glanced at him, a frown creasing her forehead. "I'm just doing my job, Gregg. The mirror might be a lead we've overlooked."

Gregg raised an eyebrow. "Since when did you start taking urban legends seriously?"

Before Sarah could respond, the front door creaked open. Samuel Blackwood, a tall man with a big puffy beard in his mid-forties with a weathered face and piercing eyes, appeared in the doorway. His expression was a mix of curiosity and apprehension.

"Good evening, Mr. Blackwood," Sarah said, trying to sound professional despite her unsettled nerves. "I'm Detective Sarah Lawson, and this is Officer Gregg McAlaney. We're here to follow up on some questions regarding a mirror you tried to buy from the Crestfall museum."

Blackwood's eyes flickered with recognition. "Ah, the mirror. Come in, please." He stepped aside, allowing them to enter. The interior of the house was dimly lit, with antique furnishings and heavy curtains that muffled the sounds from outside.

As they stepped into the living room, Sarah's unease grew. The room was filled with odd trinkets and relics, each telling its own story of mystery and the arcane. Sarah's gaze wandered around, noting the collection with a mix of intrigue and discomfort.

"Mr. Blackwood, can you tell us why you were interested in the mirror?" Gregg asked, breaking the silence. "And why didn't you end up buying it?"

Blackwood settled into a worn armchair, his eyes narrowing slightly. "The mirror intrigued me because of its history. Legends and folklore often have a kernel of truth, and I wanted to explore that. But when I learned the owner of the museum was reluctant to sell it, I decided it wasn't worth pushing."

Sarah shifted uncomfortably, feeling the weight of her own conflicted feelings about the case. "You mentioned in your inquiry that you believed the mirror had some significance. Can you elaborate?"

Before Blackwood could respond, Sarah's phone buzzed. She glanced at the screen—a phone call from the person she least expected–Jenny. Her attention briefly diverted, memories of her past flooding in, Sarah felt a pang in her heart, scared to answer the call. She missed Blackwood's intense scrutiny. Gregg noticed the phone call, and wondered who it was. However, Sarah muted the call.

As Blackwood began to speak, Gregg nudged Sarah subtly. "You sure you're alright? You're more invested in this mirror than usual."

Sarah's eyes met Gregg's, and she opened her mouth to explain her sudden curiosity. But before she could formulate her thoughts, Blackwood's voice cut through the room. "It seems I've piqued your interest, Detective. I hope it's not just idle curiosity."

Sarah was momentarily taken aback by the directness of Blackwood's statement. She was about to answer when Gregg interjected, "Actually, we're here to uncover the truth behind these stories. Anything you can tell us about the mirror's history might help us find Jessica Smith. She's a teenage girl missing; her friends say she was taken by the mirror."

Blackwood nodded slowly, his gaze shifting to the mantelpiece where an old, dusty book lay. "Very well. The mirror is said to have been a gift given to a little girl named Raven Wondersun in 1955 by her abusive father. The story goes that Raven was going to expose her father's affair to her mother and the mirror was a gift for Raven to keep her mouth shut. However, when Raven stood her ground, her father beat her to death in front of the mirror to keep his secret." Blackwood said as he shifted his gaze back to Sarah and Gregg, "Since then, she haunts the mirror and reveals the darkest secrets of those who stand in front of it."

Sarah exchanged a glance with Gregg. The information was unsettling but also seemed to align with the disturbing images she had seen earlier.

"You believe these stories are true?" Sarah asked, her pulse quickening.

"Sometimes the truth lies beyond our understanding. However, do I believe it's real? That's a tricky question. I've seen enough to know that sometimes, reality and legend blur in ways we can't always explain. Whether the mirror is truly haunted or just a vessel for our fears, it seems to have a power that defies easy answers. The real question is, why do you want to know? What are you hoping to find?"

Sarah's mind started racing. The reflection she'd seen earlier—the haunting image of the oil and stool—came back to her with renewed intensity. "I—I just want to find the people that have gone missing," Sarah said, her hands beginning to tremble. The case was taking a turn she hadn't expected, and her disbelief was being challenged in ways she hadn't anticipated.

"Thank you for your time, Mr. Blackwood," Sarah said, standing up. "We might need to follow up with you again. Your insights have been... enlightening."

Blackwood nodded, a faint smile playing on his lips. "I look forward to hearing from you two again."

As Sarah and Gregg left the house, the evening chill seemed to deepen, mirroring the growing unease in Sarah's mind. She knew she had to confront her own doubts and fears as she continued her investigation. The boundary between the plausible and the impossible was becoming increasingly blurred.

As Sarah got into the driver's seat and Gregg settled in the passenger seat, Gregg stopped her. "Stop it, what's going on?" he said, trying to get her to open up about her sudden interest in the case.

Sarah became nervous. "Wh—What do you mean?" she said, a sweat forming on her brow.

Gregg stood his ground. "I mean, what is with this? I've known you for two years, and you've always hated paranormal stories. You said, 'I don't believe in that shit.'" He was trying to make sense of Sarah's newfound interest. "Look, I'm all up for stories, hell, I watch so many horror TV shows, but we need to find Jessica Smith."

Sarah took a deep breath, looking straight ahead. "This is going to sound fucking nuts, but I need you to bear with me. I swear I saw a reflection in the mirror that wasn't me."

Gregg started to laugh a little, caught off guard by Sarah's admission. "Come on, Sarah. You? Seeing things in haunted mirrors? That's a new one."

"Humor me," Sarah said, her tone serious. "What did you see?" Gregg asked, still chuckling but more curious now.

"I saw something from my past," Sarah said quietly, her eyes fixed on the road. "Something bad that happened to me a long time ago. Just like how the legends describe the mirror."

Gregg's laughter faded as he saw the intensity in Sarah's eyes. "Okay, let's say I believe you for a moment. What does this mean for the case?"

"It means there might be some truth to these legends," Sarah replied. "I don't know how or why, but we need to dig deeper. If the mirror can show me my past, maybe it really did something to Jessica."

Gregg sighed, his reluctance evident. "Sarah, this is... I don't know. It's hard to believe, and I'm not sure chasing ghost stories is going to help us find Jessica. We should report to Captain Wilson."

Sarah looked at him, her expression firm. "No! He's going to tell us to drop the case." She said, "We need to at least try, we have to explore every possibility. Let's go back to the station and look into Raven Wondersun. Maybe her story can give us some clues."

Gregg hesitated, clearly uncomfortable with the idea. "Alright, Sarah. I'm in. We've been partners for a while, and I trust your instincts, even if I don't believe in ghosts. But, I'm telling you right now, as soon as this thing goes south, I'm calling it off."

"Thanks, Gregg. It means a lot," Sarah said, a cheesy smile playing on her lips as she started the car. As they set out for the station, Gregg couldn't shake his skepticism. He had agreed to help Sarah, but he wasn't convinced that the mirror was haunted or that Sarah had truly seen something. However, he knew he didn't want to disappoint his partner. He also knew that he might have to bring her back to reality if this took her over the edge.

Sarah focused on the road, her mind racing with thoughts of Raven Wondersun and the mirror's dark history. Gregg glanced at her, his reluctance to fully believe still nagging at him, but he pushed it aside for now. They needed to find Jessica, and if this was the way to do it, he would follow Sarah's lead.

As they pulled into the station parking lot, Gregg took a deep breath, steeling himself for what was to come. "Alright, let's dig into Raven Wondersun's past and see what we find," he said, trying to muster as much enthusiasm as he could.

"Thanks, Gregg. I know this isn't easy to swallow," Sarah replied, her determination unwavering.

4 - The Wondersun Family

Gregg sat with Sarah as they researched Raven Wondersun and her family. The dim light from the computer screens cast an eerie glow on their faces as they sifted through old records, newspaper clippings, and archives. The silence between them was punctuated only by the occasional rustle of paper or the soft click of a mouse.

"This is going to take us all night," Gregg muttered, rubbing his temples. "There's so much to go through."

Sarah, focused and determined, ignored his complaint. "We'll find something. We have to."

Hours passed, and the stack of documents grew taller. Finally, Sarah stumbled upon a particularly old newspaper article. "Here, look at this," she said, pointing to a yellowed clipping. The headline read: "Tragic Death of Young Girl in Crestfall: Raven Wondersun Dies in Horrific Domestic Incident."

Gregg leaned in closer to read. "It says here she died in front of the mirror, just like Blackwood said. Her father was suspected but never charged due to lack of evidence."

Sarah's eyes widened as she read further. "Listen to this: 'Neighbors reported hearing strange noises and seeing unusual reflections in the mirror in the days following her death.'"

Gregg sighed. "So, the legends about the mirror might have some basis in fact after all."

Sarah nodded, her mind racing. "We need to find more about her family, especially her father. If we understand what happened back then, it might give us clues about Jessica and where she is."

Gregg pulled up another file, this one containing census records. "Here we go. Her father's name was Arthur Wondersun. Looks like he stayed in Crestfall for a few years after Raven's death but then moved away. No record of him after that."

Sarah frowned. "What about her mother?"

Gregg shook his head. "No mention of her mother in any of these records. It's like she disappeared from history."

As they continued the investigation, Gregg glanced up at Sarah. "Sarah, back in the car, you said the mirror reflected something that happened to you a long time ago," Gregg said, realizing how little he knew about his longtime partner. "We've been working together for two years. You know my favorite coffee. You even fuckin' know where my parents live."

Sarah looked up at Gregg, disturbed and angry. "And?" she snapped, trying to shut down the conversation.

"Look, all I'm saying is that I've known you for a while, and you never talk about your parents or if you have any siblings," Gregg insisted.

Sarah's emotions cut through her words. "Gregg, drop it. I don't want to talk about this right now," she nearly yelled.

Gregg backed off, realizing it was a touchy subject for Sarah. "Sorry, I didn't mean to intrude," he said, looking back down at the newspapers. Sarah quickly realized how rude she had been. "Look, I'm—I'm sorry. I've never told anyone this."

Gregg's gaze remained on the newspaper. "It's okay," he said softly, feeling a little embarrassed and annoyed that Sarah had yelled. Sarah felt embarrassed and sorry that she let her emotions pierce through Gregg. "I grew up outside Crestfall, in San Antonio," she said as Gregg raised his head again. "I had a great family: Dad was a mechanic, Mom was a teacher. It was me, them, and my sister, Jenny—"

Gregg cut Sarah off. "Jenny? She was calling your phone at Blackwood's residence."

Sarah began talking again. "I haven't spoken to her in six years," she said, her voice choking a little. Gregg noticed this. "Hey," he said, trying to comfort her, "What happened?"

Sarah wiped away a single tear. "When I was 17, my dad died," she said, the memories threatening to break her. "And it was my fault."

Gregg's eyes widened. He hadn't known that his partner had gone through so much. "I'm so sorry, Sarah."

She continued her story. "He was working on the car, and I saw a puddle of an oil leak and I didn't tell him. He lit a cigarette and—" Sarah's eyes filled with fresh tears. "His whole body broke into flames," she said, her voice finally breaking. "I don't know, maybe if I was better, maybe if I told him about the leak," she said, wiping her tears, "Maybe he'd still be here."

Sarah calmed herself down. "That's why I became a detective. I can't forget what I did. Maybe I could be better and stop shit like this. I don't know."

Gregg looked down, realizing why his partner was so obsessed with this case. Why she was so adamant in believing the legends surrounding the mirror. It touched something deep within her, a wound she had never fully healed from.

Gregg placed a reassuring hand on her shoulder. "You've done a lot of good as a detective. Look, I know it's hard, but you've got to let go. You can't change what happened, but we can decide how it shapes us going forward." Sarah took a deep breath, appreciating Gregg's words. "Thanks, Gregg."

As they sifted through the newspapers and documents, piecing together the history of the mirror and its victims, they found a common thread. Each person who had come into contact with the mirror had a deep, personal trauma, something that haunted them more than any ghost could.

"Do you think the mirror is somehow feeding off people's pain?" Gregg asked, voicing the thought that had been forming in both their minds.

Sarah nodded slowly. "It's possible. Maybe that's why it's so powerful. It reflects not just our images but our deepest fears and regrets."

Gregg glanced at Sarah, his skepticism slowly eroding. "Alright, so what's our next move? We have more information, but how does this help us find Jessica?"

Sarah leaned back in her chair, deep in thought. "We need to find an address. If the mirror is truly connected to all this, maybe there's something we missed. Something that can tell us where Jessica is."

Gregg hesitated. "Sarah, this is a long shot. We're basing everything on legends and old stories."

Sarah met his gaze, her resolve unwavering. "I know it sounds crazy, but it's the only lead we have. We owe it to Jessica's grandmother to follow every possible clue, no matter how far-fetched it seems. You saw how much pain she was in."

Gregg sighed, knowing she was right. "Alright, let's get an address. But Sarah, if this whole mirror business turns out to be nothing, we need to look at more conventional leads."

"Deal," Sarah agreed, grabbing her coat.

Gregg opened his laptop and searched up the address of the Wondersun family. The family had lived outside of Crestfall. "1017 Westcreek Blvd. Holy shit, the house looks like a haunted mansion now."

Sarah peered at the screen over Gregg's shoulder. The picture showed a dilapidated old house, its windows boarded up and the yard overgrown with weeds. "Well, that fits the bill," she said dryly.

"Are you ready for this?" Gregg asked, closing the laptop and grabbing his keys.

Sarah nodded, determination in her eyes.

The drive to 1017 Westcreek Blvd was tense and silent. The sun had set by the time they arrived, the house looming ominously in the twilight. They parked the car and approached the front door, which creaked open with a gentle push.

Inside, the air was thick with dust and the scent of decay. Shadows danced in the corners as their flashlights swept through the rooms. It was clear no one had lived there for years, but the sense of foreboding was palpable.

"Let's split up," Sarah suggested. "We can cover more ground that way."

Gregg hesitated but nodded. "Alright, but stay in touch. Yell if you find anything."

As they searched the house, Sarah found herself drawn to a room at the end of a long hallway. The door was slightly ajar, and she pushed it open to reveal what must have once been a young girl's bedroom. Faded wallpaper with cartoon animals adorned the walls, and a small bed sat in the corner, covered in dust.

She moved to the closet, her heart pounding. Inside, she found a small wooden box. Opening it, she discovered a collection of old photographs and letters. One photograph caught her eye—a family portrait of a man, a woman, and a young girl. The girl looked strikingly like the pictures of Raven Wondersun they had seen.

Sarah flipped through the letters, her eyes scanning the faded ink. One letter, in particular, stood out. It was from Arthur Wondersun, addressed to an unknown recipient. The letter was filled with desperate pleas and cryptic mentions of the mirror and its power.

Meanwhile, Gregg was exploring the basement. The air was colder here, and the sense of unease grew stronger. He stumbled upon an old trunk, and inside, he found journals and notebooks filled with Arthur Wondersun's handwriting. They detailed journal entries and rituals involving the mirror, hinting at a dark obsession.

Gregg's flashlight flickered, and he heard a faint whispering. He turned quickly, but saw nothing. Shaking off the chill, he continued reading. One passage mentioned a hidden room in the house, where Arthur conducted his experiments. The journal indicated that the room could be accessed through a secret door in the basement.

"Sarah," Gregg called out, his voice echoing through the house. "I found something. Get down here."

Gregg stood in the dimly lit basement, the air heavy with the weight of years of secrets. "Sarah," he called out again, more urgently this time. "I found something. Get down here."

Sarah hurried down the creaky stairs, flashlight in hand. "What is it?" she asked as she reached Gregg, who was standing by the trunk filled with Arthur Wondersun's journals.

"Look at this," Gregg said, handing her one of the journals. "It talks about a hidden room where he researched his so-called rituals and kept his journal entries. The entrance is supposed to be somewhere in this basement."

Sarah scanned the page, her eyes widening. "A hidden room? We need to find it."

They began searching the basement, tapping on walls and moving old furniture. After several minutes, Sarah noticed a section of the wall that sounded hollow. "Gregg, over here," she said, pointing to the spot.

Gregg joined her, and together they pushed against the wall. It gave way, revealing a narrow passage hidden behind it. "Help me open this," Sarah said, her voice tinged with excitement and apprehension.

With a bit of effort, they managed to pry open the hidden door, revealing a dark corridor that led deeper into the house. They exchanged a glance before stepping through.

At the end of the corridor, they found a room filled with papers covered in dried ink and an old voice recorder from the

1940s. The air felt even colder here, the sense of dread more pronounced.

Sarah moved quickly, scanning the notes scattered around the room. "Gregg, look at this," she said, holding up a entry. "Raven's dad felt immense guilt after her death. He believed the mirror was reflecting her and started looking into dark magic to bring her back. He thought she was trapped beyond some dimensional barrier."

Gregg listened, his skepticism waning as he absorbed the implications. "So, you think maybe the mirror pulled him in? That he's still in there somehow?"

"Maybe," Sarah replied, her voice steady despite the gravity of her words. "It explains his disappearance. And if Raven—or whatever this thing is—can pull people in, it could have taken Jessica too."

Gregg's eyes fell on the dusty, rusted voice recorder. He wiped it clean and tried to play it. At first, it refused to turn on, but after a few taps, it whirred to life, startling them both.

The recording began with the voice of an out-of-breath and distraught man. "Arthur Wondersun, August 14, 1955. Recently, the house has begun to emit paranormal activity. It's my dearest Raven; it has to be. I've seen her in the mirror. It is my fault she is there, thus I must get her out."

Gregg hit the next recording. "Damn it, Raven has begun to get mad whenever I approach the mirror, throwing objects around the house. The ritual Blackwood gave me requires a sacrifice. I—I have to. For Raven."

Sarah interrupted, "Wait, Gregg? He said Blackwood?" Her curiosity was piqued. "Mr. Blackwood knows more than he's letting on," Gregg said, switching to the last recording.

Arthur's voice crackled through the speaker. "I am confronting the mirror. Raven? Raven! There you are, my sweet little girl. Come home to me. I am sorry. I am so sorry. I won't hurt you anymore. Just please—come home to me."

Suddenly, Arthur's voice turned to screams, a horrifying sound that made both Sarah and Gregg jump. The recording ended abruptly, leaving a chilling silence in its wake.

Gregg turned off the device and looked at Sarah, his face pale. "Sarah, I don't know—"

"You promised," Sarah cut him off. "You promised you would humor me and try."

She took a deep breath, steadying herself. "Look, Gregg, this is even more proof. We need to go back to Blackwood. He clearly knows more than he told us. We have to find Jessica."

Gregg nodded, seeing the determination in Sarah's eyes. He knew they had to find Jessica, but his belief in the paranormal was still shaky. Yet, with everything they had discovered, he couldn't deny there was something more to this case than met the eye.

5 - Sins of Our Fathers

After locating the hidden room, Sarah and Gregg made their way back to their car. The drive was quiet, each lost in their thoughts about the chilling discoveries they had just made. The moonlight cast eerie shadows on the road, mirroring the unease they felt.

When they arrived at Blackwood's residence, it was well past midnight. The mansion loomed in the darkness, its imposing presence more ominous now that their investigation had taken such a disturbing turn. As Sarah and Gregg approached the front door, Sarah's phone started ringing again, she took it out and it was her—Jenny was calling again. Sarah's heart felt heavier, why was Jenny calling her after all these years? Sarah couldn't answer it, she had been away for so long and there was no way her mom and Jenny would forgive her. Sarah muted the call once again and looked to Gregg, "Your sister again?" He asked. Sarah nodded and proceeded to ring the doorbell.

The doorbell chimed loudly, breaking the silence. Blackwood answered, his face showing surprise and concern at the late hour.

"Detectives," he greeted, his voice cautious. "What brings you back so late?"

"We've found something significant," Sarah said, her voice urgent. "We need to talk."

Blackwood led them into his study, a room lined with shelves of books and faintly illuminated by a single desk lamp. He gestured for them to sit, though both Sarah and Gregg remained standing.

Gregg took out his notebook and began. "We discovered recordings from Arthur Wondersun. He mentioned dark rituals and a sacrifice. There was also a reference to someone named Blackwood."

Blackwood's eyes widened slightly, but he quickly composed himself. "Arthur Wondersun was indeed a client of my father's. I'm familiar with the name, but I didn't know the full extent of his dealings."

Sarah leaned in. "We need to understand what you know. If Arthur was looking into dark practices and rituals involving the mirror, it might be connected to Jessica's disappearance."

Blackwood looked troubled. "My father did have Arthur as a client, but he was never deeply involved with the mirror itself. He was concerned about its influence and tried to stop Arthur from pursuing such dangerous paths. Unfortunately, he couldn't prevent Arthur from becoming obsessed."

Sarah raised her voice a little, "Why didn't you tell us this from the start? This was obviously why you were interested in purchasing the mirror."

Blackwood's eyebrows raised, "Detective, would you have believed a middle aged man rambling about a haunted mirror?

Wait—why are the two of you so interested in this? The police discard these types of stories."

Sarah looked down, a sweat forming on her brow again, remembering the horror she had seen in the reflection of the mirror. Samuel's expression widened, "The mirror, it showed you its power, didn't it?" He said, noticing Sarah's distress.

"I—" Sarah was struggling to explain what she saw. However, Gregg interrupted them, Gregg raised an eyebrow. "Okay wait, So your father knew about Arthur's interest but didn't realize the extent of it?"

"Exactly," Blackwood said. "My father wanted to halt Arthur's dangerous research but didn't have the means to intervene completely. Arthur's obsession grew beyond what he could control, and my father was left feeling helpless."

Sarah's expression softened. "So you're saying your father tried to stop him but didn't succeed?"

Blackwood nodded. "Yes, my father believed the mirror was a conduit to something dangerous but didn't understand its full power. He wanted to prevent its misuse, but Arthur's desperation led him down a dark path, and my father was the type of man, who after payment would not care."

Sarah and Gregg exchanged glances. "Do you have any information that could help us?" Sarah asked. "We need to find Jessica, and the mirror seems to be the key."

Blackwood sighed. "I can share what my father knew and any documents he left behind. It might not be much, but it could help you understand how to approach the mirror and its dark influence."

Gregg nodded. "We're willing to take whatever you can provide. We need to find Jessica and stop this."

Blackwood stood up, looking resolute. "I'll gather the relevant materials. But please be careful. Dealing with the mirror is fraught with danger, and it's not something to be taken lightly." He said, looking at Sarah, "Especially when it has given you a taste of what it can do, Detective Lawson."

Samuel then proceeded to get his father's journals and the two sat down on the chair. Gregg remembered Jenny's call, "Look Sarah, I know I am in no position to talk to you about this but don't you think you should call her back? Jenny, I mean. I mean if she's calling you after this long, it's gotta be important, right?"

Sarah responded with hesitation, "No—no, I can't. It's been too long, I—No, forget about it." She said getting up. Sarah leaned against the wall, staring at her phone like it was a dangerous animal. "Gregg, you don't get it," she said quietly, her voice shaking. "When I left, I didn't just move away—I ran. I ran from my family, my sister, my mom... I abandoned them. I've been gone for years without a single word. They must hate me for disappearing, for not being there when they needed me most. What if they can't forgive me for that? What if calling her just rips open old wounds that never healed? I don't know if I can face that shit."

Gregg looked at Sarah with a mix of compassion and determination. "Sarah, you can't keep punishing yourself forever. People make mistakes, and yeah, you left, but you did what you thought you had to do at the time. Maybe Jenny's reaching out because she needs you now, or maybe she just wants to reconnect. You won't know until you try. And even if it's hard, even if it hurts, isn't it worth it to know? To at least try and make things right? Family is fuckin' complicated, but they're still *your* family."

Sarah looked down at her phone at her recent calls directly at Jenny's name, then she looked back up, "I—I can't." She said, her eyes welling up.

Blackwood then walked back into the room, his hands full with his father's journal entries. "Here it is." He said, placing them on the desk. He walked over to his chair, and sat. "So? Are we going through these?" He asked. Sarah and Gregg looked at each other then at the papers, and sighed. They all proceeded to go through all of it.

Many hours passed, and the sun began to rise. Gregg had fallen asleep, his head resting on the desk. Sarah looked over at Blackwood, feeling a bit embarrassed. "Sorry about—," she said, pointing to Gregg, referring to his current state.

Blackwood chuckled warmly. "Ha! Don't worry, when I started, this work would drop me to sleep within minutes."

Sarah's curiosity was piqued. "What is it exactly that you do? You said Arthur was your dad's client. What work was your dad doing?" Blackwood's strange home and peculiar profession had confused Sarah.

Blackwood sighed and leaned back in his chair. "My father ran a supernatural agency, believe it or not. People would come to us with their paranormal problems, and we would fix them. At least, that was the idea."

Sarah's eyes widened. "A supernatural agency?"

Blackwood nodded. "Yeah, but it wasn't all noble work. Eventually, my father got lazy. He only did it for the cash. He'd perform half-hearted rituals, make promises he couldn't keep.

When I told him that we could be helping people better and more by actually giving a damn and trying, he brushed me off."

Sarah frowned. "So, you took over after he passed away?"

"Exactly," Blackwood said, his expression turning serious. "Ever since he passed away, it's been up to me to fix his mistakes and improve on this place. I couldn't stand seeing people suffer because of his negligence. It's why I've dedicated my life to genuinely helping those who come to me."

Sarah nodded, understanding the weight of Blackwood's responsibility. "So, Arthur Wondersun came to your father for help with the mirror?"

Blackwood nodded slowly. "Arthur was desperate. He believed the mirror had trapped his daughter's spirit. My father took his money but didn't truly help him. It's one of the many failures I've been trying to make right."

Sarah glanced at Gregg still sleeping, then back at Blackwood, "It's just—I don't get it." She said. Blackwood turned back to Sarah, "Get what?" He asked.

Sarah looked down at the journal entries, Arthur loved his daughter so much. However, he was the one that delivered the blow that killed her. "If Arthur really loved his daughter, why did he kill her?" She said.

Blackwood looked at a picture in his office of him and his father, "Fear. Fear of his affair getting out. Fear of his family viewing him differently." He said as he held the frame in his hands, "When you love someone, you try your hardest not to make mistakes. But the truth is, love itself is full of mistakes." He said. Sarah noticed that Blackwood related to it.

Gregg stirred and lifted his head from the desk, blinking groggily. "Did I miss anything?" he asked, rubbing his eyes.

Sarah shook her head. "No, not really. We've gone through the entries. They mostly confirm what we already know."

Gregg sat up straighter, looking at the scattered papers. "So, what's the plan now?"

Blackwood leaned forward, his expression serious. "From what we've read, my father, Richard Blackwood, was hired by Arthur Wondersun to free his daughter's spirit from the mirror. Arthur became obsessed, and while my father initially tried to stop him, he eventually gave up once he was paid."

Sarah added, "But there's also a ritual detailed in the entries. It's supposed to free the spirits trapped in the mirror."

Gregg frowned. "So, what do we need to do?"

Blackwood pointed to the journal. "We need to go to the museum and perform the ritual. The mirror is still there, and the ritual, if done correctly, might free Jessica and stop whatever is controlling it."

Sarah glanced at Gregg, a mix of determination and apprehension in her eyes. "We have to try. This is the only lead we have."

Gregg nodded, standing up and stretching. "Alright then. When do we do this?"

Blackwood stood up as well, gathering the journals and notes. "As soon as possible. The longer we wait, the more dangerous it becomes."

The trio prepared to leave, gathering the necessary materials for the ritual. The sun was fully up now, casting a harsh light through the windows. The sense of urgency was palpable as they headed back to the car, ready to face the mirror and whatever dark forces awaited them at the museum.

As they drove, Gregg glanced at Sarah. "You okay?" he asked softly.

Sarah nodded, though her eyes betrayed her anxiety. "Yeah. Just thinking about everything. And Jenny."

Gregg placed a reassuring hand on her shoulder. "We'll get through this, Sarah. And afterward, maybe you can call her. One step at a time, okay?"

Sarah managed a small smile. "Okay. One step at a time."

6 - Reflection

The car came to a stop outside the museum, the vehicle's headlights casting long shadows as the three stepped out into the chilly night air. Sarah, Gregg, and Blackwood approached the grand facade of the museum, its stone steps illuminated by the moonlight. The silence of the night was only broken by the crunch of gravel underfoot.

As they walked up the long and lengthy stairs of the museum, they were greeted by Tyson Lackson. His weary eyes met theirs with a mix of surprise and curiosity. "Evening, detectives," Tyson said, attempting a warm smile that didn't quite reach his eyes. "What brings you back here so late? Again,"

"We need to close the museum for a while," Sarah replied firmly. "We're working on something and need complete privacy."

Tyson's eyebrows knitted together in concern, but he ultimately complied, locking the doors behind them. The trio moved with purpose through the dimly lit corridors of the museum, their footsteps echoing softly off the walls. They reached the room housing the mirror, its darkened form casting an unsettling aura even in the subdued lighting.

Sarah's heart pounded as she entered the room. The mirror stood before them, its surface a haunting expanse that seemed to swallow the light. The memories of the horrific vision she had seen in the mirror came rushing back, filling her with dread. She hesitated, her feet feeling as though they were glued to the floor. The mirror's dark allure was almost tangible, and she struggled to summon the courage to step closer.

Gregg turned to Blackwood before he started the ritual, "Blackwood, what does this ritual do exactly?" He asked. Blackwood opened his book, "If done correctly, this ritual should release all souls trapped within the mirror, alive or dead."

Blackwood wasted no time. He began setting up the ritual, spreading a circle of salt around the mirror with practiced precision. He placed a dog's collar bone at specific points, followed by sprinkling cinnamon and pepper. The mixture of scents filled the room, adding to the ritual's eerie atmosphere. With a steady voice, Blackwood recited a long Latin incantation, his words filling the space with an ancient, haunting cadence.

Sarah waited, she thought about Jessica and her grandmother, and how happy Jessica's grandmother would be to see her again.

As Sarah and Gregg stood by, their anticipation grew. They braced themselves for the room to erupt into chaos—objects flying, the mirror distorting. But the minutes ticked by in silence. The room remained eerily calm, the mirror's surface was completely undisturbed. Sarah's heart raced with anxiety and confusion. She glanced at Blackwood, who looked as composed as ever.

"Did you do it right?" she asked, her voice trembling slightly.

Blackwood's eyes met hers, steady and calm. "Yes, the ritual was performed correctly."

Gregg's frustration was evident. He looked around the room with a growing sense of defeat. "This entire thing was a waste of time. We should report to Captain Wilson and explore more practical leads."

"No," Sarah retorted, her voice sharp with determination. "We need to try again, do more research. You promised me you'd try."

Gregg's patience snapped. "I did try. We did. But nothing's happening. Blackwood's father never even confronted the mirror directly, and how do we know that Arthur actually saw something in the mirror, he was grieving, maybe he saw something that he took out of context. We need to follow a different lead."

Sarah's anger flared. "No, I'm the detective here. You don't get to decide what lead we follow. We're going to keep trying."

Gregg's eyes widened in shock at Sarah's harsh tone. He felt the sting of her words, his own frustration boiling over. "Alright, fine," he said tersely. "I'm going to make a call."

Five minutes later, Gregg returned, his face a mask of resolve, and a little bit of guilt. "We need to head back to the station. We can do more research there, see if we can uncover something useful. Blackwood, we'll contact you if we need any more information."

Blackwood nodded, his expression a mix of concern and understanding. "I'll be here. I'll see if I missed anything. Please be careful."

As Sarah and Gregg left the museum, the night air seemed heavier, laden with the weight of their failed attempt. The drive back to the station was filled with an uneasy silence. Gregg was unusually quiet, his gaze fixed on the road ahead. Sarah, sensing his mood, turned to him with a mixture of guilt and concern.

"I'm sorry for yelling," she said softly. "Are you okay?"

Gregg sighed deeply, his exhaustion evident. "I'm just burned out. This whole case... it's wearing me down. I didn't expect it to be this tough."

They arrived at the police station and they entered the front door. As Sarah walked to her office, she noticed that everyone was giving her stares, judgmental stares. "What's going on?" Sarah muttered to Gregg. Gregg remained silent. As she entered her office, Sarah noticed Captain Wilson waiting in her chair, a stern expression on his face. "Captain?" she asked, her surprise evident.

Wilson looked up from the desk with a grave demeanor. "McAlaney informed me about the Jessica Smith case. Given everything that's happened, I'm placing you on a month's leave. It's crucial for you to address your personal issues and mental health."

Sarah's heart sank. She looked to Gregg with disappointment, and betrayal. "I'm fine. I can handle it. I don't need time off."

Wilson's expression remained stern. "That's an order, Lawson. We can't have detectives diving into the supernatural. It isn't real. Look, you've been here for a while and have done a lot of good for us, but I know when someone is grieving; If something happened to you, you need to take the time and heal your wounds."

Sarah's anger boiled over. She grabbed her bag and stormed out, her face flushed with rage. She collided with Gregg on her way out, her frustration palpable. "Fine!" she snapped, her voice raw with emotion.

Gregg watched, his heart heavy with guilt. Gregg felt like he had no other choice but to tell Captain Wilson, but the guilt of betraying his partner heavied his heart. Wilson placed a reassuring hand on his shoulder. "You did the right thing, Gregg. I know you'll solve the case. We're counting on you."

Sarah arrived at her apartment, her emotions in turmoil. She unlocked the door and slammed it shut behind her. The familiar surroundings offered little comfort as she stood in the middle of her living room, overwhelmed by the weight of her failures. She looked at her coffee table which had a picture of her and her family, she picked it up, running her hand across the frame. She couldn't hold it in anymore, everything she did, she failed at. Her dad's death, her leaving her family behind, failing to find Jessica. She threw her bag to the floor and collapsed to her knees, her sobs wracking her body.

The pain was relentless—Each failure seemed to crush her spirit further. She hit the floor with her fists until they were bloody, her tears mingling with the blood. Her sobs were fierce, each cry a release of the anguish she felt.

Exhausted and emotionally drained, she eventually fell asleep in a pool of tears and blood. Her dreams were plagued by the traumatic night of her father's accident. The flames, the searing pain, intensified her suffering. The pressure was unbearable as she begged for forgiveness from Jenny and her mother, her heart racing with fear and desperation.

In the dream, as she pleaded, her mother and Jenny vanished, leaving her alone in a void of sorrow. She was left alone, the silence echoing the emptiness she felt inside. Sarah woke up in the early hours, her face streaked with dried tears and blood, her heart heavy with the weight of her dreams and her waking reality. Sarah had nothing left—no answers, no hope, no purpose—just nothing.

7 - The Weight Of Loss

FOUR WEEKS LATER

Sarah woke up to the oppressive silence of her apartment, the weight of the past four weeks pressing down on her. Since she was placed on temporary leave, the days had blended into a haze of regret and self-loathing. She dragged herself out of bed and made her way to the kitchen, the morning light filtering weakly through the blinds.

She grabbed her medication from the counter, the pills meant to keep the nightmares at bay, and washed them down with a gulp of tequila. The burn in her throat was a familiar comfort, numbing the edges of her guilt and mental pain. The betrayal by her own partner, Gregg, was a wound that refused to heal. She poured another shot and downed it, hoping for a few moments of peace.

Slumping onto the couch, Sarah flicked on the TV. The news blared, "The search for Jessica Smith still continues as Officer Gregg McAlaney leads the case." Her grip tightened on the remote, and she quickly turned off the TV, muttering under her breath about Gregg's betrayal and how she should be the one leading the case.

As she lay back, wallowing in self-pity, her phone buzzed. She squinted at the screen, rubbing her eyes to see more clearly. It was her therapist, Dr. Joanna Christene. Sarah groaned and picked up the call.

"Yes, Dr. Christene?" she mumbled.

"Sarah, you're late for your session. Are you on your way?" Joanna's voice was gentle but firm.

Sarah sighed. "I'll be there in twenty minutes."

After hanging up, she groaned again, feeling the weight of yet another obligation. She begrudgingly got ready and drove to Dr. Christene's office, her thoughts swirling with anger and self-doubt.

The drive felt like an eternity, filled with memories of better days and the sharp sting of her current failures.

Finally, she arrived at the building and took the elevator to the seventeenth floor. Room 07 loomed ahead, and she walked in, greeted by the familiar sight of Dr. Christene's warm smile.

"Sarah, come in," Dr. Christene said, motioning to the chair. "How have you been feeling?"

Sarah collapsed into the chair, rolling her eyes. "I hate this, Joanna. Captain Wilson didn't need to put me on therapy."

"He wants what's best for you, Sarah. He wants you to come back to work as soon as possible."

Sarah huffed. "If he wanted what's best, he wouldn't have put me on leave in the first place."

"Let's talk about how you've been feeling," Dr. Christene prompted. "Have the nightmares been any better?"

Sarah nodded reluctantly. "The medicine helps, but they're still there."

"Have you been doing the breathing exercises we practiced?" Dr. Christene asked.

"Yeah, yeah," Sarah muttered, eyes drifting to the clock.

The therapist wrote something down, then looked up at Sarah with a thoughtful expression. "Let's talk about your father."

Sarah's heart clenched at the mention. She hated talking about him, especially after Gregg had betrayed her trust. "The weight of loss is overbearing and what happened to you was tragic, but it wasn't your fault," Dr. Christene continued.

"If I'd told him about the leak, he'd still be alive," Sarah whispered.

"You couldn't have known that would happen," Dr. Christene reassured her. "Look, I notice in a lot of my clients that reconnecting with family can lead to healing. Maybe it's time to reach out to your sister and mother."

"I can't," Sarah said, her voice hollow. "They won't accept me."

"Jenny tried to contact you weeks ago. Maybe she wants to reconnect. You'll never know if you don't try."

The session ended, and Sarah found herself back in her apartment, she dove into her couch, the weight of the day pushing her down. She thought about what her therapist said, Sarah didn't want to feel like this anymore.

She picked up her phone, scrolling through her recent calls until she found Jenny's name. Her heart raced as she hesitated over the call button, then noticed a voicemail.

With trembling hands, she clicked on voicemail. Sarah didn't know what Jenny had to say, maybe something about how bad of a sister Sarah was, how she's been gone for so long.

Sarah clicked on it and played the message. "Hey, sis," Jenny's voice came through, bringing fresh tears to Sarah's eyes. It had been years since Sarah had heard her beautiful sister's voice. "I don't know if you still use this number, but... God, I don't know what to say. It feels like I should be mad at you, but honestly, I—I miss you. So much has happened since you left. I got married, had kids..."

Sarah choked back a sob as she listened. "Anyways, sorry. The reason I called is that... Mom's... gone." The words hit her like a punch to the gut. "We're holding the funeral next Tuesday. Please come if you're free. She loved you, Sarah."

The message ended, and Sarah was left staring at her phone, tears streaming down her face.

She had missed her mother's funeral. "Fuck!" she screamed, the pain overwhelming her. The guilt was unbearable, but she couldn't stay frozen in her grief. She checked the date on the voicemail—four weeks ago. Without thinking, she grabbed her keys and rushed out of her apartment, determined to at least visit her grave.

THREE HOURS LATER

The drive to San Antonio Cemetery was a blur, her mind replaying the voicemail over and over. She pulled up to the entrance, the sky cloudy and threatening rain. Walking through the cemetery, she searched for her mother's headstone. Finally, she found it, right next to her father's.

Together in life, together in death.

Sarah fell to her knees, her heart breaking all over again. "There's nothing I can do. I left you guys, and I couldn't save you, Dad. I could have come back sooner, I—I could have at least apologized to you, Mom. I could have told you how much

I missed you, how long I've been yearning to talk to you again. And now I'll never get the chance." Her voice broke as she sobbed, "I love you. I love you, Mom and Dad. I want you."

A snap of a branch behind her made Sarah look up. It was her, she had a new messy bun hairdo, she was dressing differently, and was taller, but it was her, Jenny.

Sarah stood, wiping her eyes, lost for words. "Jen..." she whispered. Jenny's eyes filled with tears as she smiled.

"Sis." Jenny let out.

They ran into each other's arms, collapsing to the ground, sobbing together.

8 - Rainy Reunion

As they sobbed in each other's arms, the weight of years apart and unspoken words melted away in the rain. For the first time in so long, Sarah felt at peace, happy even. Jenny's embrace was warm and comforting, a stark contrast to the cold and gray life that Sarah had led.

As Jenny retracted from Sarah, she punched Sarah in the arm. "If you fucking run away like that again, don't bother coming back!" she said ferociously, then hugged Sarah tightly again. Sarah's arms tightened around Jenny; she never wanted to let go again. "I'm sorry. I'm so sorry, Jen," Sarah said, all her troubles fading away with the simple hug.

They both retracted, and Jenny looked at their mother's grave. "Mom—Mom, she wanted me to let you know that she loved you, that before she died, she forgave you."

Sarah looked at her mother's grave, thinking about all the memories she had with her, and how she couldn't even show up for her funeral. "I wish I was here. I'm sorry I wasn't here. I was scared if I called, you guys would tell me to fuck off and that you wouldn't forgive me, and that I was a bitc—"

Jenny put her hand on Sarah's lips. "Stop—It's okay. Sure, we have a lot to talk about but... It's okay." Jenny's hand retracted from Sarah's lips. The words "It's okay" washed relief and happiness over Sarah. She had thought about her family and how they felt about her for so long. To hear that Jenny and her mother forgave her was a happiness that she had been craving for so long.

Jenny helped Sarah up, and they proceeded to the nearest bench. They talked for hours about Teena's silly antics, and how funny, sweet, and kind their mother was. They reminisced about their memories together and how much they loved her. As they talked, Sarah looked down in gratitude. She had never been the religious type, but she felt compelled to say, "Thanks, God." Jenny then tapped her on the back. "Yo, I know a new spot that opened up here recently. It's called Jim Nortons. Their fucking iced coffee is amazing. Come, let's go," Jenny said as she got up. Sarah got up with her, saying, "Yeah, let's do it. Lead the way, I'll follow behind."

They walked over to their vehicles and got in. Sarah followed Jenny to Jim Nortons. After about ten minutes, they arrived there. As they got out of their vehicles and entered the shop, they both ordered a vanilla iced coffee with an extra pump of vanilla. They sat down and began drinking. "Mmm, fuck, this shit is good," Sarah said, looking up at Jenny. Jenny laughed, enjoying the moment. "I told you so."

Sarah smiled at Jenny. "Jen, you have no idea how much I've missed you. I've always wanted to call and do stuff like this." She took another sip. Jenny took a sip and looked up at Sarah. "So, why didn't you? I mean, I've missed you so much. But, why didn't you call at all?" she asked. Sarah felt a pang in her heart, thinking about her time away and their father's death. "I know I've said this a lot today, but I'm sorry. After

Dad died, it really fucked me up. I blamed myself. I thought moving away would help me get better. It—It only made me feel even more like shit."

Jenny looked up in concern as she took another sip of her iced coffee. "Why would it be your fault? No one knew about the gas leak. When Dad lit the cigarette and started to smoke it in the car, no one knew what happened would happen." Jenny said. Sarah thought about the incident and how she saw the leak. "*I* did," she said, looking down in shame. "That day, Dad asked me to get his phone from the garage. I bent over to get his phone on the stool, and I saw gas leaking from underneath the car. Fuck, I was so fucking stupid. I thought Dad was working on something and left it as is. If I told him, he'd still be here." The trauma of the incident pierced through her words. A tear dropped from Sarah's eyes, but she rubbed it off; she had done a lot of crying and was tired. Jenny took and held Sarah's hands in her own, trying to be a source of comfort. "Hey, it's alright. You were a teenager, you couldn't have known," she said, tightly holding Sarah's hands.

"I was 17. I should have used my fucking common sense and told Dad about it," she exclaimed. Jenny tried to reassure Sarah. "But you didn't. You can't change the bad shit that happened in the past, but we can stop it from letting it control our lives today. What happened to Dad wasn't your fault; nothing you can say will make me think it was your fault."

Sarah smiled as another wave of comfort and relief washed over her while she held Jenny's hands. She had been dreaming about this for years, and it was finally real.

Jenny got up, taking her coffee with her. "Come, I have some people who are dying to meet you," she said as she began to walk outside. Sarah's confusion flared. "Who?" she asked. Jenny looked back. "You'll see, just come!" she exclaimed. As Sarah got out of her seat, her phone started buzzing in her pocket. She took it out and looked at the caller ID—it was Gregg. Sarah looked at the name and thought about his betrayal and how he sold her out. She muted it as she ran behind Jenny.

They both got into their vehicles, and Sarah followed behind Jenny once again.

TWENTY MINUTES LATER

After twenty minutes, Sarah and Jenny arrived at a single house complex. They both got out, and Sarah followed Jenny. "Where are we? Whose house is this?" Sarah asked as Jenny took out her keys for the front door. "Sis, shut up and you'll see," Jenny said as she unlocked the door and proceeded inside. Sarah stood frozen outside; she had forgotten that in the voicemail, Jenny mentioned she had a family now. Sarah got nervous about the idea of having nieces and nephews. She didn't think she was the greatest role model. "You coming?" Jenny said as she stood by the door. Sarah shook it off and walked inside.

Suddenly, she heard the sound of two children running down the stairs—two girls. "Mommy!" the girls excitedly said in unison. They reached the ground floor and tightly hugged Jenny. Sarah couldn't help but let a tear drop down from her eye, realizing how beautiful Jenny's daughters were. She quickly cleaned it off. The two girls looked toward Sarah, and the slightly taller, straight-haired girl's eyes shot up in confusion. "Mommy, who is this?" she asked, looking up at Jenny. Jenny bent down on her knees, eye level with her tallest daughter.

"Jolie, Mary, this is your Auntie Sarah," she said, smiling up at Sarah. The look on the two girls' faces turned from confusion to happiness. They both then ran to Sarah, giving her a tight hug around the legs. "Auntie Sarah!" they both exclaimed. "Mommy told us so much about you."

Sarah was a little hesitant as she looked at Jenny while her daughters hugged her legs. Jenny signed to her, letting her know it was okay. Sarah bent down on her knees, hugging them back. "She did, huh?"

The two then retracted, and the little one, Mary, began speaking. "Auntie Sarah, is it true that when you were a teenager, you stole Grandma's car to go meet a boy?" she excitedly asked. Before Sarah could answer, the oldest one, Jolie, started talking. "Is it also true that you almost got arrested for speeding?" she exclaimed. Jenny got in between the two of them. "You two, relax. She just met you," Jenny said. Sarah looked up at Jenny, smiling. "No—No, it's—it's okay," she said to Jenny. She shifted her gaze to Mary. "Yeah, I stole Grandma's car to meet a boy. He was so cute," she said. She then shifted her focus to Jolie. "Haha, no, I don't know what your mom is talking about me getting arrested," she said as she laughed with Jenny. Mary jumped in excitement. "What was his name?" she asked, the excitement of a two-year-old pouring through her veins. "His name was Ferguson Davison," Sarah replied. A look of disgust washed over Jolie and Mary's faces as they looked at each other, then back at Sarah. "Ew! What kind of name is 'Ferguson'?" Jolie said. Sarah started laughing. "Haha, yeah, I don't know. I guess cute boys have the ugliest names," she said as the two kids started laughing. Mary had another question. "Also! Also! Auntie Sarah, can you teach me how to use makeup? Mommy won't let me," she asked.

Jolie looked at her, pushing her away. "No! Me first!" she exclaimed. Mary got back in the front, angry. "Why do you get to learn first?" she asked with frustration on her face.

The fighting reminded Sarah of her and Jenny, and how they used to bicker and fight.

"Because I'm older than you!" Jolie exclaimed. Mary's voice got a little louder. "You're only... uh... This much older than me!" Mary said as she held one finger up. Jolie then lightly shoved Mary. Jenny held their arms and separated them. "You two, cool it now!" she yelled a little. "Listen, you two are—"

Sarah interrupted Jenny. "—Sisters, you have to watch out for each other," Sarah said, remembering her father's words from all those years ago. Jenny smiled but returned her focus back to the kids. "You can't be fighting. Go watch TV while I talk to Auntie Sarah," she said as the two ran off.

Sarah smiled at them running off, then looked back to Jenny. "I never imagined it. You have children, much less me having nephews or nieces," she retorted.

"I've told them a lot about you. They love you," she exclaimed. More footsteps came running down the stairs. It was a man with short hair, mild stubble, and muscular. "Hey Sarah, this is my husband, Johnny," she said as she gave him a kiss on the lips. "Hey. My wife has told me a lot about you. I hear you're great," he said, nodding at Sarah. "Thanks," Sarah said, surprised that Jenny had been mentioning her a lot.

"If you guys will excuse me, I have to go to the office to pick up some things," he said, standing by the door. Jenny gave him another kiss. "Okay, bye honey," she yelled, while he left for the car. Sarah chuckled. "Damn, sis, you hit yourself the jackpot," Sarah exclaimed. Jenny looked up to her in confusion. "What do you mean?" she asked. Sarah looked at the car as it came out of the driveway and onto the road. "Where does he work?" Sarah asked. "Dealership. San Antonio Auto."

"Wow, rich *and* handsome. Good stuff, sis," she exclaimed. Jenny started laughing. "Don't worry, you're not the only one who got it in them."

As Sarah stood by, enjoying the comfort of being with family, her phone started buzzing again. Sarah took it out and saw it was him again—Gregg. "Hey Jen, I have to take this really quick," she said as she walked outside, closing the door behind her. "Okay," Jen said.

Sarah stood in the night and cold air. She pressed the answer button and held the phone to her ear. "You got a lot of nerve calling me—"

Gregg interrupted her. "Look, I'm sorry, and I'll make it up to you. But we have a problem and I need you right now!" Gregg yelled. Sarah yelled back. "Relax! Relax! What's going on?!"

"You were right! About everything! About the mirror! I need you because... things just got worse."

9 - Haunted Mirrors & Gregg

Sarah stared at her phone, Gregg's words echoing in her mind. She felt the chill of the night seep through her jacket as the warmth of Jenny's home became a distant memory. The sudden urgency in Gregg's voice pulled her back into a reality she had hoped to escape, even if just for a little while.

"About the mirror," she muttered to herself, feeling a knot tighten in her stomach. The mirror had been a source of contention, a symbol of everything that had gone wrong. She took a deep breath and looked back at the house, the laughter of her nieces faintly audible through the closed door.

For a moment, she considered going back inside, pretending Gregg's call had never happened. She longed to hold onto the fleeting sense of normalcy. But she knew better; ignoring the problem wouldn't make it go away. She had to face it, even if it meant dragging herself back into the darkness she had been trying to escape.

"Hold on, Gregg," she said, her voice steady despite the turmoil inside her. She ended the call and walked back into the house.

Jenny looked up from the couch where she was sitting with her daughters. "Everything okay?" she asked, concern evident in her eyes.

Sarah hesitated for a moment, then took a deep breath. "Jen, there's something I need to tell you. I'm a detective. That call was from the station. They need me on a case."

Jenny's eyes widened in surprise. "A detective? Why didn't you tell me?"

"I didn't want to worry you," Sarah replied. "I know that I've been away for a long time, and I promise I'll come back and visit regularly. But I really have to go now. It's important."

Jenny's apprehension was clear, but she nodded. "Alright. Just... be careful, okay?"

Sarah smiled and hugged her tightly. "I will. Save my number, and call me anytime."

She gave her nieces one last hug before heading out the door. As she got into her car, her phone buzzed with another call from Gregg. She answered it and put the phone on speaker as she drove. "Where are you right now?" Sarah asked as she pulled out of Jenny's driveway. Gregg quickly replied, "In your apartment."

"Why the fuck are you in my apartment?" She angrily said, the emotions of the past four weeks finally piercing through her. "Sorry–Sorry, I know I fucked up, But shit is fucking nuts recently."

Sarah calmed herself down as her curiosity piqued, "What's going on?"

Gregg's voice came through, tense and hurried. "Okay, so this began two days ago..."

FORTY-EIGHT HOURS EARLIER

Gregg sat down on the chair in Sarah's old office, the familiar surroundings only serving to amplify his frustration. For the past four weeks, he had been trying to find Jessica Smith, but to no avail. Leads had dried up, witnesses had gone silent, and the few clues they had seemed to lead nowhere. The frustration had been bubbling up, and frankly, Gregg didn't know where to take the case next.

He stared at the cluttered desk, remnants of Sarah's meticulous work habits still evident. He had hoped that stepping into her space would bring some inspiration, some insight into the elusive case, but so far, nothing.

The door creaked open, and Captain Wilson walked in, his expression a mixture of concern and expectation. "Gregg," he said, closing the door behind him, "Any updates on Jessica Smith?"

Gregg sighed, running a hand through his hair. "Not much, Captain. I've followed every lead, questioned everyone who might know something, but it's like she vanished into thin air. I don't know where to go from here."

Captain Wilson leaned against the desk, folding his arms. "This case is a high priority. We need to find her, and soon. There has to be something we're missing. Have you gone through all of Sarah's old notes? Maybe there's a connection we overlooked."

Gregg nodded. "I've been through them multiple times. Sarah was thorough, but there's nothing concrete to go on. I'm starting to think we need a fresh perspective."

Captain Wilson raised an eyebrow. "What about Sarah herself? She's been gone for a while, but she had a knack for seeing things others missed. Could she help?"

Gregg hesitated. "Sarah's been through a lot, Captain. You put her on leave for a reason. I don't want to pull her back into this."

Wilson's gaze hardened. "We're running out of options. If Sarah can help, we need to bring her in. This case isn't just another missing person. There's something bigger at play here."

Gregg sighed, knowing the captain was right. "Alright, I'll consider it."

Wilson nodded. "Do what you have to do. Just keep me updated." The captain said as he left the office.

Gregg stared at his phone, contemplating whether to call Sarah. The memory of her anger and the betrayal she felt because of him weighed heavily on his conscience. He had sold her out, and the guilt gnawed at him every day. His finger hovered over her contact, but he couldn't bring himself to press it.

Lost in his thoughts, he was jolted by the sudden ring of his phone. The caller ID displayed an unknown number. Reluctantly, he answered, "Hello, this is Gregg."

The voice on the other end was familiar but unexpected. "McAlaney? It's me, Samuel. Blackwood."

Gregg's brow furrowed in confusion and annoyance. "Blackwood? Why are you calling me?"

Blackwood's voice was urgent. "I've found new information that could provoke the mirror and finish the ritual."

Gregg sighed, his frustration evident. "We already tried a 'ritual,' Blackwood. This whole haunted mirror business is not real. It's a wild goose chase, and I'm not wasting any more time on it."

Blackwood's tone grew more insistent. "If you don't believe it, then don't come to my office tonight at 10. But I'm telling you, this is different. This is real."

Gregg shook his head, anger bubbling up. "Blackwood, you're a waste of time. If you call me again with this nonsense, I'll have you arrested for obstruction."

He ended the call abruptly, tossing his phone onto the desk in frustration. As much as he wanted to dismiss Blackwood's ramblings, a small part of him couldn't shake the nagging feeling that there might be something to it. But with Sarah still a fresh wound in his mind, he couldn't afford to chase a dead end that they have already chased.

Gregg looked around the cluttered office once more, hoping for a spark of inspiration. The case files, Sarah's old notes, and the scattered evidence seemed to mock him. He needed a breakthrough, and he needed it soon.

Deciding he had to try something, Gregg thought back to his earlier interactions with Jessica's grandmother. She had been distraught, but also the only consistent figure in Jessica's life. Maybe she knew something that hadn't come up before, something that could provide a new lead.

He grabbed his coat and headed out, determined to visit Mrs. Smith. The drive to her house was filled with a mixture of hope and apprehension. He didn't want to disappoint her again, but he needed to exhaust every possible lead.

Gregg parked in front of the modest house and approached the door, knocking gently. After a moment, the door opened to reveal Mrs. Smith. Her face lit up with recognition, despite the lines of worry etched deeply into her features.

"Officer," she greeted, her voice a mixture of surprise and warmth. "You're the tall and handsome one. Come in, come in."

Gregg managed a small smile as he stepped inside. "Thank you, Mrs. Smith. I'm sorry to come by unannounced, but I wanted to check in and see if there's anything new you might remember about Jessica."

They moved to the living room, and Mrs. Smith gestured for him to sit. She settled into a chair across from him, her expression turning somber. "I wish I had something new to tell you, Detective. I think about Jessica every day, but it's like she just vanished. I've been praying for her, hoping for a miracle."

Gregg nodded, understanding her pain. "We're doing everything we can to find her, Mrs. Smith. I know it's been a long time, but we're not giving up."

Tears welled up in Mrs. Smith's eyes, and she dabbed at them with a tissue. "I understand if the police need to focus on other cases. It's been so long, and I know you have so many people to help. I just... I just want to know she's safe, wherever she is."

Gregg looked down, guilt gnawing at him. He had promised Mrs. Smith he would find her granddaughter, and so far, he had failed. He leaned forward, trying to convey his sincerity. "Mrs. Smith, don't give up hope. When times are tough, that's when we have to hold on even tighter. I believe we'll find her. We just need to keep pushing."

Mrs. Smith managed a weak smile through her tears. "Thank you, Detective. That means a lot to me."

Gregg stood, feeling a renewed sense of determination. "I'll do everything I can, Mrs. Smith. I promise."

As he left her home, Gregg couldn't shake the feeling that time was running out. He had to find Jessica, not just for the case, but for her grandmother's sake.

Gregg looked at his phone as he walked outside, thinking and hesitating about calling Sarah again. As he debated with himself, he glanced at the time: 9 o'clock. He remembered Blackwood's call earlier and looked back at the house. Jessica's grandmother had lost hope, and Gregg knew he had to give it back to her.

"I have to be on another level of batshit crazy to go through with this," Gregg muttered as he set the GPS to Blackwood's estate. He got in the car and headed out. During the thirty-minute drive, he thought about Sarah again. If he called her, she would probably cuss him out and refuse to come back. "I'm so fucked," he thought, imagining how mad Sarah must have been.

After some time, Gregg finally pulled along the curb of Blackwood's estate. He stepped out of his car and proceeded up the steps. He knocked on the door and waited for what seemed like ages. Blackwood finally answered, and Gregg, already frustrated, snapped, "What took you so long?" as he walked in.

Blackwood had a smirk plastered on his face. "So, you decided to come?" he asked, leading Gregg to his office.

Gregg sat down, contemplating the absurdity of going through with the ritual. "Look, Blackwood, we need to find the girl. We tried this before, and it didn't work. I thought it was all fake. But when I saw how hopeless her grandmother was... I—We need to try everything, even if it's—"

Blackwood prompted him, "Say it," chuckling.

Gregg rolled his eyes and sighed. "Even if it's paranormal."

Blackwood then sat down and opened his journal. "So, I figured out why the ritual didn't work when you and your colleague visited the estate," he said, looking up at Gregg. "By the way, where is Lawson?"

Gregg's face darkened at the mention of Sarah. "Lawson is dealing with her own shit right now. She's not coming."

Blackwood raised an eyebrow. "Shame. She was the one who seemed to have the connection."

Gregg leaned forward, his patience wearing thin. "Just tell me why it didn't work."

Blackwood nodded and turned a few pages in his journal. "The problem was the location, the number of people involved, and the fact that they need to be in the mirror. The mirror is a gateway to another dimension, but it requires the collective will of many people to open fully. Specifically, it needs a balance of energies: half of the people need to have faced a dark past, carrying pain and regret, while the other half need to hold hope for a bright future, filled with belief and optimism. It's a kind of cosmic balance."

Gregg scoffed. "You want me to believe that we need a bunch of people with mixed baggage to make this work?"

Blackwood's expression turned serious. "If you want to find Jessica, you need to let go of your skepticism. The mirror responds to belief, to energy. It requires a balanced group to channel the necessary power, and they all need to be in the same location, specifically within the dimension of the mirror."

Gregg rubbed his temples, feeling a headache forming. "Alright, let's say I believe you. How did you find this information?"

Blackwood leaned back, a hint of pride in his voice. "I went over my father's notes again. He had a recorded conversation with Arthur Wondersun about the ritual. It's a long shot, but it's one we need to take."

Gregg nodded slowly, still processing the information. "I don't even know where the hell to start looking for these people."

Blackwood closed his journal and looked Gregg in the eye. "We start with those closest to the case. Jessica's family, her friends, anyone who has been affected by her disappearance. We also need people who believe in a better future, who have hope despite everything. And we need to find a way to get everyone into the mirror's dimension."

Gregg sighed. "This sounds insane, but I think I know some people who might fit the bill."

Gregg settled in with his laptop, looking through old newspapers and social media posts, trying to piece together a list of Jessica's friends and influential figures in Crestfall who might fit the necessary criteria. Hours passed, and Gregg fell asleep at his laptop around 7 AM, exhausted and frustrated by the lack of progress.

TWENTY-FOUR HOURS EARLIER

At 6 PM, he woke up with a start. Blackwood, noticing his disheveled state, cracked a joke. "If you're going to be sleeping here often, I'm going to start charging you. This isn't the first time, Officer McAlaney."

Gregg apologized and shook off his sleepiness. Just then, his radio crackled to life. "Officer McAlaney, we got a code 10-62, ongoing break-in at the Crestfall Museum. Near you."

Gregg looked at Blackwood, eyes wide. "Hop in," he said, rushing out to his car.

At the museum, Amy and Danny, masked and armed with bats, navigated through the dark corridors. Danny expressed his apprehension, but Amy reassured him. "It's gonna be okay. We're doing this to get Jessica back."

They found the room with the mirror and approached it nervously. Amy took a deep breath and yelled, "Give Jessica back! Now!" Danny joined in, but the mirror remained silent. Desperation setting in, they began slamming their bats against the sides of the mirror.

As Gregg and Blackwood arrived on the scene, Gregg joked, "How am I not gonna get fired for this?" referring to bringing Blackwood along to a break-in.

They rushed inside, heading to the room where Amy and Danny were attacking the mirror. "Danny? Amy?" Gregg called out, recognizing them. "Don't!"

Amy retorted, "You didn't believe us, so we have to get Jessica back ourselves." Suddenly, the room began to shake softly, then violently. The mirror distorted, and a glass-like hand reached out, pulling Amy in despite her struggles. Danny stepped back in fear.

Everyone broke into a sweat as fear almost overwhelmed all of them. Blackwood panicked and rushed to help Amy, grabbing her arm. But the mirror's strength began to pull him in as well. Amy screamed, and Danny tried to help, but Gregg pulled him back. "Stop! You'll get pulled in too!"

As Blackwood was being pulled in, Gregg yelled, "Why the fuck would you do that?"

Blackwood shouted back, "Find Lawson! Bring everything we used last time!" His final words before him and Amy being fully pulled in were, "I'm depending on you."

Gregg rushed Danny out to his car, his mind racing. He knew he needed to get to Sarah.

PRESENT

"And then, I came to your apartment just now." Gregg said to Sarah on the phone. Sarah left speechless and profounded of the last 48 hours' events.

"So, the kid, Danny, is with you right now?" Sarah asked, still driving back to Crestfall. Gregg looked over at Danny who was sitting on the couch, with sadness and guilt plastered on his face, Gregg knew Danny felt guilty for not being able to save Amy. "Yeah, he's here."

"I'll be there in one hour." Sarah firmly said, she knew that she had to try to stop the mirror and save everyone that was lost, and try not to die trying.

10 - Broken Bridges

After an hour, Sarah finally arrived back in Crestfall, her thoughts still revolving around her reunion with Jenny and Crestfall's haunted mirror. As she contemplated her future—whether to move back to San Antonio or leave her detective career behind—she walked up to her apartment.

She opened the door to find Gregg trying to comfort Danny on the couch. Danny was sobbing, the weight of guilt over not saving Amy clearly heavy on him. Sarah entered, and both Gregg and Danny noticed her. Danny quickly wiped his tears, while Gregg stood up, a hint of nervousness in his posture.

Gregg hadn't spoken to Sarah in a while, and the strained relationship was palpable. "What do we do now?" Sarah asked, her gaze shifting to the grieving Danny. Gregg met her eyes. "Blackwood said we need to gather the same materials from the last ritual and go inside the actual mirror."

Sarah shook her head in frustration and walked to the kitchen cabinet. "I've been keeping this stuff in case we needed it again," she said, angrily slamming the items onto the table.

The tension in the room was thick. "Look, Sarah, I'm sorry—" Gregg began, but Sarah cut him off. "No, I don't want to hear anything from you right now," she said, slamming her hand on the table. "I can't deal with this right now." As she headed to her room to grab something, Gregg attempted to reach out to her but was interrupted again.

"You know," Sarah said, reappearing with a dog's collar bone, "I'm not even mad that you went to Captain Wilson. Sure, I yelled at you, and maybe I was out of line. But what really pisses me off is that I opened up to you about my shit, and you went and told Wilson everything." She paused, her anger evident. "You sold me out because you didn't believe in the supernatural crap. And now that you do, you're asking me for help? What a fucking hypocrite."

Gregg's frustration boiled over. "I'm sorry for selling you out, but how did you really fucking expect me to believe in a haunted mirror?" He shot back, his voice tense. "I've made mistakes, and yes, I told Wilson things I shouldn't have. But you can't fault me for asking for us to follow leads that seemed more fucking rational at the time. We needed to solve this case, and I didn't see another way."

Sarah's anger piqued even more, she was nearly at her boiling point, "What are you tryna say? I'm a bad detective?" She asked as her fists closed up. Gregg stood his ground as his fists closed as well, "Maybe."

Sarah and Gregg stood in the middle of the room, their argument escalating as if they were about to brawl. They were interrupted by Danny, who shouted furiously, "STOP!" He stood between them, his face a mask of anger and determination. "I don't give a fuck about your issues right now! Jessica, Amy, your friend—they're in the mirror! So stop squabbling like a fucking married couple and calm the fuck down!"

Sarah and Gregg exchanged glances, the tension between them easing as they recognized the urgency of the situation. Sarah took the dog collar bone and placed it in a bag along with the cinnamon, pepper, and salt. She held up the bag and nodded for Gregg to head to the museum with her.

"Wait, I'm coming too," Danny interjected.

Gregg shook his head. "Kid, you're going to get hurt. Stay here, and we'll try to get everyone home."

Danny stood his ground, his voice firm. "No, fuck that. My friends are in there, and I couldn't save them before, but now I have a chance."

Gregg's eyes softened slightly, but he remained firm. "Danny, this isn't a game. It's dangerous, and you're not equipped for it."

Danny's resolve didn't waver. "I'm not letting them down again. I'm going."

Seeing Danny's determination, Sarah glanced at Gregg. "We don't have time for this. Let him come. We need all the help we can get."

Reluctantly, Gregg nodded. "Alright, but stick close and stay out of the way. We'll try to get in and out as fast as possible."

As they prepared to leave, the weight of their mission was heavy on all their shoulders. They knew the risks but understood that they couldn't afford to let fear or old grievances stand in their way.

They all stepped into Sarah's car, the atmosphere inside heavy with the gravity of their mission. As Sarah drove towards the museum, the silence was thick with tension, each of them wrestling with their own fears—whether of the mirror itself or the unknown horrors within it.

After a tense fifteen minutes, they arrived at the museum and got out of the car. Danny broke the silence with a joke, "Hey, Romeo, Juliet, are we going in or what?"

Sarah shot back, "Buddy, it's not like we fight a haunted mirror every day." They began walking up the stairs, and Gregg chuckled, catching Sarah's glance. It was a fleeting moment of connection, a small sign of forgiveness.

With the ritual tools and baseball bats in hand, they entered the museum and made their way through the dimly lit hall toward the room with the mirror. Each step felt like an eternity, the silence growing more oppressive.

As they reached the room, Gregg stepped up to the mirror, but once again, nothing happened. "So, what now? Last time, hitting it made it react. Any new ideas?" he asked, his voice echoing in the empty room. Sarah and Gregg scanned the room for anything that might trigger the mirror.

Suddenly, a noise filled the room—the sound of liquid pouring. Sarah's heart raced, her mind flashing to unsettling memories of her father's death. Gregg's eyes widened as he peered into the mirror. "No, I—Fuck," he muttered.

"What's wrong?" Sarah asked, her voice tight with concern.

"It's something from *my* past," Gregg replied, his face pale. The mirror reflected an eerie scene—a fence with a toy truck and blood seeping from the fence.

Without hesitation, Gregg extended his finger towards the mirror. It rippled like liquid mercury as he pushed his whole hand through, then stepped in. Sarah followed immediately, determined to face whatever awaited them. Danny hesitated for a moment, then muttered, "This is the smartest fucking idea ever," as he nervously stepped into the mirror.

11 - Into the Abyss

Trauma is a shadow that follows you, no matter how fast you run or how far you go. It lingers in the corners of your mind, waiting for the quiet moments to remind you it's still there. You can try to bury it, mask it, or pretend it doesn't exist, but the truth is, you'll never truly escape it. Trauma isn't something that disappears because you ignore it; it festers, it grows, and it seeps into every aspect of your life. The more you run from it, the more it consumes you from the inside out.

Your secrets, the things you hide, they have a way of surfacing. They don't stay buried forever. You might think you've locked them away, that you've hidden them so deep that no one will ever find them. But secrets have a life of their own. They gnaw at you, they distort your reality, and eventually, they come to light. And when they do, they bring with them all the pain, all the guilt, and all the fear you thought you'd left behind.

Running doesn't solve anything; it only delays the inevitable. You can't outpace the truth. Sooner or later, you'll have to face what you've been avoiding. And when that time comes, the weight of everything you've tried to escape will crash down on you all at once. It's not a question of if, but when. And when that moment arrives, you'll realize that the only way to truly be free is to confront what haunts you, no matter how terrifying that may be. Because the alternative is to live a life ruled by the shadows, always looking over your shoulder, waiting for the day when your past catches up with you.

"Hello!" Danny screamed, his voice echoing into the void. He stood in the center of a vast, black abyss, illuminated only by a single flickering lightbulb suspended above him. "Mr. McAlaney! Ms. Lawson! Where are you?!"

His heart pounded in his chest, each beat resonating with his mounting fear. The oppressive darkness pressed in on him from all sides, suffocating and endless. He could barely see his own hands, let alone any sign of an exit. The silence was deafening, broken only by his own frantic breaths.

Danny's mind raced with thoughts of what could be lurking in the shadows. He was terrified—not just of the black nothingness surrounding him, but of the unknown dangers it might conceal. Every creak and whisper in the darkness sent shivers down his spine. He desperately hoped for a response, a glimmer of hope that he wasn't alone in this nightmarish void. But as the moments dragged on, the silence remained unbroken, and Danny's fear grew ever more suffocating.

Suddenly, a piercing scream shattered the silence. Danny's head snapped towards the sound, his heart skipping a beat. Without a second thought, he sprinted towards the source, hope surging within him. "Wait, I'm coming!" he yelled, his voice cracking with desperation.

As he ran, the darkness seemed to close in around him, but he pressed on, driven by the need to find McAlaney or Lawson.

In the distance, he spotted a figure standing with their back turned. Danny's breath caught in his throat as he recognized the familiar clothing. "Jessica?" he called out nervously, his voice trembling.

The figure remained still, unresponsive. Danny's steps slowed as he approached, dread coiling in his stomach. He reached out a tentative hand, his fingers inches from her shoulder. "Jessica?" he repeated, his voice barely a whisper.

Suddenly, the figure snapped around, revealing Jessica's face—scarred, bruised, and twisted with anguish. "It's your fault! You didn't save me! Why didn't you save me?!" she screamed, her voice filled with pain and accusation.

Danny stumbled backward, his legs giving way beneath him. He fell to the ground, scrambling to back away from the haunting apparition. "I'm sorry!" he cried, tears streaming down his face. "I'm so sorry!"

Jessica's figure loomed over him, raising a hand as if to strike. Danny cowered, covering his head with his arms, bracing for the blow. But nothing happened. He waited, trembling, then slowly lowered his arms and opened his eyes.

The figure was gone. The oppressive silence returned, leaving Danny alone once more in the abyss. He took a shuddering breath, his heart still racing, the encounter leaving a deep, chilling fear in his soul.

Danny's heart pounded as he scanned the darkness. In the distance, a solitary door stood, illuminated by the soft glow of a street lamp. He cautiously made his way toward it, every sense on high alert. Once he felt the path was clear, he dashed through the door, bursting into a new scene.

Inside, Danny was horrified to see Gregg suspended in the air, his eyes rolled back, glowing white. The mirror nearby seemed to be the source of this torment, forcing Gregg to relive his past trauma. "Please, no! Aunt Claire!" Gregg cried out in agony.

Danny rushed to Gregg's side, desperately trying to pull him down. "It's not real! Come on, I need you guys!" he shouted, shaking Gregg. When that didn't work, Danny slapped him hard across the face.

Gregg snapped out of the trance and fell to the ground with a thud. Rubbing his cheek, he glared up at Danny. "Don't ever do that again!"

Before Danny could respond, a dark, demonic, female-like voice echoed through the room. "Danny Colton, Gregg McAlaney. It was a dumb idea coming here."

The two men froze, their fear palpable. Gregg, summoning a burst of courage, yelled out, "What are you?!"

The voice responded with a chilling, demonic laugh. "I am the shadow that lurks in the corners of your mind, the whisper that haunts your restless nights. I am the darkness you've tried to bury, the truth you fear to face. I am the reflection in the mirror that shows you who you really are, not who you pretend to be. I am your reckoning, the one who strips away your lies and reveals the secrets you thought were safe. I am the harbinger of your worst fears, the keeper of your darkest truths. I am inevitable."

The room seemed to darken further, the atmosphere growing heavier with each word. Danny and Gregg exchanged terrified glances, realizing they were up against something far more sinister than they had imagined.

Danny helped Gregg up as they once again scanned the darkness. Danny once again saw a door with a street lamp. However, the door was more classical, like something from the fifties. "There." He pointed to the door. They walked over to the door and opened it, they opened it to see a familiar surrounding, Blackwood's office. However, it was more clean, more organized. An older man having a striking resemblance to Samuel came through the door, "No, it doesn't matter Samuel! He already paid in cash." He yelled out, as he crashed into his chair. A young Samuel Blackwood came through the door, "Father, you're leaving Mr. Wondersun into an obsession that will swallow him." He exclaimed.

His father pulled back in his chair, not giving the biggest damn, "It's not like I forced him to investigate the mirror."

Little Samuel's face expressed a very angry and frustrated look, "We have the power to help by actually giving a damn!" He ferociously yelled.

His father bounced out of his chair, furious, "Watch your tone, boy." He firmly said. Samuel astounded, tried getting his point across, "But—"

"No buts! Go to your room! Now damn it!" His father yelled even louder. Samuel looked down in frustration and anger, he then noticed something to his right, he looked down then directly met Gregg's eyes, "McAlaney?" He asked. It was like he was shaking off a trance. "Blackwood?" Said Gregg, confused. "What the hell was that?" He asked, Samuel's father now standing frozen.

Samuel's heart pumped, "The mirror. It's forcing us to relive our biggest regrets." He said still shaken of his memory,

"Everytime I've shaken off the trance, the memory restarts, and I'm back in the trance."

"Let's bounce then!" Danny exclaimed as he opened the door that they came from.

As they walked through the door, suddenly, they were on a street with all every house down the street in darkness, and only one with the lights on. Danny, Gregg, and Samuel made their way to the house with the lights on. They all carefully made their way up the steps of the bright house, unsure of what they were going to discover. Gregg carefully opened the door into the house and they found a woman cooking. Their nerves started racing, wondering what this was, Danny stayed behind while Gregg stepped forward, to get her attention, she interrupted him.

"Sarah! Jenny!" The woman called, "Dinner's ready!"

"Coming!" Two girls shouted back in unison. One girl bounded down the stairs, then the other closed on her heels. Sarah grabbed her plate and stood in line, a smirk on her face as she waited for their mother to serve the food.

"Sarah?" Gregg called out, confused, but no answer. "Hey! Why do you get food first?" Jenny protested, trying to push her way to the front.

"Because I'm older," Sarah declared, her smirk widening.

Jenny rolled her eyes. "Relax, sis, you're only two years older than me." She gave Sarah a playful shove, but Sarah held her ground.

"I'm 17," Sarah retorted, "I'm basically almost an adult."

Gregg tried getting the little Sarah's attention again, "Sarah! Come on! It's not real!" He yelled out again. However, again she didn't respond.

Their father, Tom, walked into the kitchen, his clothes smeared with grease from working on his car. "Keyword: almost," he said with a chuckle.

Gregg's eyes widened as he looked at Sarah's father, knowing what this memory was of, "Who are these people?" Danny asked.

"Sarah's family." He said, "This is the day her father died."

Teena joined in, her laughter lightening the room. "If it's any consolation, you both are idiots," she teased as she placed food onto Sarah's plate first.

As Jenny stepped up for her food, she grabbed a fork and joked, "This is abuse. I'm calling CPS."

Teena looked up at Jenny, a mischievous glint in her eye. "Ha! Call 'em to take both yer' asses away."

Jenny smiled, grabbing her plate. Teena then turned to Tom. "Tom, are you hungry?" she asked as he sat down at the table.

"Yes, ma'am," he said, placing a napkin on his lap. "Load it up, please."

Teena smiled warmly at her husband. Tom then remembered something. "Hey, Sarah? Could you please get my phone from the garage? It's on the stool beside the car."

Gregg nerves pumped again, knowing the tragic end of this memory.

Sarah sprang up from her chair. "Jen, don't take anything from my plate!" she warned as she darted towards the garage.

Gregg, Danny, and Samuel followed behind, their surroundings shifting into the dimly lit garage of Sarah's memory—perhaps her darkest one. The air was thick with the pungent scent of motor oil and rusting metal. A flickering lamp cast eerie, erratic shadows across the cluttered space. Little Sarah moved cautiously, her eyes searching for the stool where her father's phone rested precariously on top.

As she bent down to retrieve it, something caught her eye—a dark, creeping stain seeping out from beneath the car. The small pool of black oil spread slowly, ominously, across the concrete floor.

Gregg couldn't bear to watch Sarah relive this trauma. He rushed forward, grabbing little Sarah's arm, attempting to pull her away from the scene. But as he did, the child's head snapped toward him, her eyes glowing with a sinister red light. "You two aren't part of this memory," she hissed, her voice cold and unnerving, her demeanor suddenly malevolent. She began advancing toward them, her steps deliberate and menacing.

They spun around to escape, but their blood ran cold as they faced older Sarah, suspended in the air, her pupils drained of color, now stark white and brimming with tears. Before they could react, they too were lifted off the ground, trapped in the air by an unseen force.

"You see, I'm a sucker for the truth," the demonic entity sneered, now wearing little Sarah's face but speaking with a voice dripping with malice. "So when people like Sarah here tell lies, I get very mad." It floated in front of the weeping Sarah, who could barely manage to mutter, "No, please..." Her voice trembled, shattered by the torment of the memory.

"So, obviously, when she got here," the entity continued with a wicked grin, "I had to—let's say—force the truth into her brain, quite literally."

"What do you want?!" Danny shouted, his voice laced with desperation. The entity's head snapped toward him, causing his heart to race with fear. "What do you want?" he repeated, his voice now trembling.

The entity cackled demonically. "Danny, it's simple. I want what everyone wants: the truth, the one-hundred percent, honest truth." It pranced back toward the car, its movements eerily playful. "Now, Gregg, Sarah told you about this memory, didn't she? How she 'found a large pool of oil under the car'?" It mocked her words with a sneer, kneeling beside the car and pointing underneath. "As you can see, it's not that large."

"What's your point?" Gregg yelled, struggling against the invisible grip holding him aloft.

The entity's voice turned icy. "Let's replay this memory, shall we? Let me show you how it really went." With a snap of its fingers, the scene rewound. Little Sarah reappeared in the garage, bending down to grab her father's phone. She noticed the small pool of oil and, in her teenage innocence, tried to tighten the cap. But her small hands fumbled, and the cap slipped from her grasp. A large stream of oil gushed out, spreading across the floor. She stood up, a chill running down her spine, but she shrugged it off, convincing herself it was no big deal.

Another snap, and they were back in the inky blackness, a single lightbulb casting a harsh glow over the group. The entity stood before Sarah, still suspended and weeping silently. "You see," it began, its voice dripping with sadistic pleasure, "that's the truly twisted thing about trauma. Sometimes, it's so unbearable, so damning, that you push it down deep—so deep that you actually start to believe your own lies. Like Sarah here, who convinced herself that the events of that day were different."

Sarah's sobs grew louder, more anguished. "Please, I'm sorry!" she cried out, her voice breaking with agony. Her dilated pupils stared blankly, forced to relive the moment that shattered her life.

The entity's lips curled into a malevolent smile, savoring her torment. "Ah, but Sarah, sorry won't change the truth, will it?"

Gregg, still suspended in the air, could feel his heart breaking as he watched Sarah suffer. Desperate to reach her, he called out, his voice filled with determination, "Sarah, listen to me! This wasn't your fault!"

The entity's sinister smile widened as it turned its attention to Gregg. "You think you can save her with a few comforting words? Pathetic," it sneered. "She's trapped, Gregg. This memory owns her. She'll never escape the truth."

But Gregg refused to give in. "Sarah, you have to fight this! Our past doesn't define who we are today! It doesn't have that power unless we let it!"

For a brief moment, Sarah's sobs faltered, as if she could hear him through the thick fog of despair. The entity's smug expression wavered, its confidence shaken by Gregg's words.

Noticing this, Danny joined in, his voice strong and unwavering. "Ms. Lawson, snap out of it!"

Blackwood gave his best too, "Come on, Lawson! We need you!" He yelled.

The entity recoiled, its grip on the memory weakening. Its eyes, still in the guise of young Sarah, flared with anger as it hissed, "You can't undo what's been done! She belongs to this pain!"

But they pressed on, their voices merging. "You're stronger than this, Sarah! You've survived everything up until now, and you'll survive this too!"

As their words pierced the air, the entity began to shudder, its form flickering and distorting. "No... NO!" it screamed, its voice echoing with rage and fear. The blackness around them rippled, and cracks of light began to pierce through.

Suddenly, the entity's body convulsed violently, and it let out a blood-curdling shriek. Its form exploded, bursting into a cloud of inky, oily blood that sprayed across the room, staining everything in sight. The oppressive darkness that had surrounded them evaporated, leaving behind only the dim light of the garage.

With the entity's temporary demise, Sarah collapsed to the ground, her body free from the invisible chains that had held her. Gregg, Danny, and Samuel dropped to the floor as well, immediately rushing to her side. Sarah lay on the cold concrete, her breath ragged, her eyes slowly regaining their color and clarity.

"Sarah, are you okay?" Gregg asked, his voice trembling with concern as he helped her up.

She looked up at them, tears still glistening in her eyes, but the terror was gone. There was only exhaustion, and a fragile hope beginning to bloom. "I... I'm so sorry," she whispered, her voice hoarse. "I was so... I didn't even realize..."

Gregg gently placed a hand on her shoulder. "It's okay, Sarah. You're here now. With me."

Blackwood looked around, confusion etched on his face. "Guys, doesn't this strike you as odd? How are we meeting each other?" He asked rhetorically. "It's like someone—or something is guiding us to each other."

Danny chimed in, "I'm not complaining. Someone's helping us." His relief was evident. However, Gregg's focus remained on Sarah, making sure she was okay as she slowly got up. "Are you okay?" he asked gently, his voice filled with concern as he helped Sarah steady herself.

She nodded, though her expression was weary. "I thought this was going to be easier," she admitted, still shaking off the dark memory that had gripped her.

Suddenly, they all blinked, and the next moment, they found themselves back in the museum room where the cursed mirror had originally been. But when they turned around, the mirror was no longer there. The room was eerily quiet, void of anything that could explain the sudden shift. They looked around, searching for clues or anyone who might be there, but found nothing.

The silence was abruptly broken by the sound of the door opening by itself, leading out of the room. "We're still inside the mirror," Blackwood reassured everyone as they cautiously walked out. They found themselves in a long, dimly lit hallway. At the end of it stood a closet, the door half-open, casting a shadow over the floor.

Their hearts raced as they slowly approached. Danny, his hands trembling, reached out for the handle. As he pulled it open, he saw something he thought he'd never see again—Jessica and Amy.

"GUYS!" he shouted, his voice cracking with emotion.

"Danny?!" they both exclaimed in unison, their faces lighting up with surprise and relief as they rushed forward, embracing him tightly. The group hug was full of warmth and the comfort of familiarity amidst the terrifying ordeal.

As they pulled back from the hug, Danny looked at Jessica, overwhelmed with emotion. "Jessica, I missed you!" he exclaimed, his voice filled with both joy and disbelief.

"Me too," she responded, her voice shaky but resolute. "I'm ready to leave now, though!"

Sarah stepped forward, feeling a sense of relief. The case she had been working on, the one that led them into this nightmare, was finally coming to a close. "Jessica, your grandmother has been worried sick about you. We're getting out of here as soon as possible," Sarah assured her.

Jessica nodded, her gaze softening as it returned to Danny. "How did you guys find each other?" he asked, still in disbelief at their reunion.

Amy and Jessica exchanged a glance before Amy spoke up. "When I got here, I landed in this room, and I saw Jessica hiding out. We've been here ever since, just trying to stay safe."

"You will not believe the shit I have seen recently," Jessica added, still visibly shaken by the horrors they had encountered within the mirror's realm.

Blackwood's eyes suddenly flickered with realization. "McAlaney," he said, turning to Gregg. "Everyone here—we're all part of the ritual. We need to stay together to complete it. The mirror's power is weakening because we're united. That's why it's been trying to separate us, to keep us from realizing this."

Gregg nodded in agreement, his mind racing. "It makes sense. The more we've come together, the more we've been able to fight back against this thing."

Gregg added, "We all need to stay focused and connected. Whatever happens next, we face it as one." He said facing towards everyone.

Sarah's eyes fixated on her bag, where she had all the ritual requirements. The weight of their importance pressed down on her.

The group continued down the dimly lit hallway, their steps echoing in the eerie silence. As they approached another door, they hesitated only briefly before opening it. Beyond the threshold was a place Sarah and Gregg recognized immediately—the ominous and decaying grandeur of The Wondersun Estate. The familiar scent of dust and old wood filled their nostrils, sending chills down their spines. Memories of their last visit to this haunted place flashed in their minds.

Sarah and Gregg exchanged a glance, both of them pale. "We're back," Gregg whispered, fear and disbelief lacing his voice. They both knew this estate too well, and the terror it held.

"We need to split up," Blackwood suggested. "We'll cover more ground that way."

Gregg, Danny, and Blackwood headed towards the basement, while Sarah, Amy, and Jessica moved cautiously up the creaking staircase to the top floor. The girls knew they had to be thorough. If there was anyone else trapped here, they couldn't leave them behind.

The top floor was dark and oppressive, each room they searched revealing nothing but dust and decay. As they reached the last room, Sarah's heart pounded. The door creaked as they pushed it open, revealing a space that seemed untouched by time—a child's room, filled with toys and fresh wallpaper. In the corner of the room, a little girl was curled up into a ball, her face hidden in her arms.

Sarah's breath caught in her throat as she recognized the child from the family portrait she had seen in the real world. "Raven?" Sarah asked, her voice trembling.

12 - Raven Wondersun

Raven looked up, her eyes wide with fear and confusion. "Please, just leave me be," she whispered, her voice trembling. "I didn't do anything wrong."

Amy and Jessica exchanged worried glances, their concern deepening. Sarah, feeling a pang of sympathy, slowly approached the frightened girl, her heart heavy. "Raven, we're not here to hurt you," Sarah said gently, crouching down to meet her eyes. "We just want to help."

Raven shook her head, her small frame trembling. "No one can help... not anymore," she murmured, her gaze flickering to something only she could see.

Meanwhile, in the basement, Gregg, Danny, and Blackwood moved cautiously through the unnaturally pristine space. "It's bizarre," Blackwood muttered, his voice echoing softly. "It's like this place is stuck in time."

They rounded a corner and came upon two old coffins, their lids slightly ajar. A heavy silence fell over them as they exchanged uneasy glances. With a deep breath, Gregg reached out, slowly lifting the lid of the first coffin. Inside, the skeletal remains of a man lay dressed in tattered clothing from the 1950s.

"I'm gonna throw up." Danny retorted at seeing the skeleton.

Gregg's breath caught in his throat as recognition dawned. "This... this is Arthur," he said in a hushed tone, his heart sinking. "Raven's father."

They turned to the second coffin, dreading what they might find. As they cautiously opened it, they were met with a sight that froze them in place: the body of a woman, eerily preserved, her features untouched by time.

"How... how is this possible?" Blackwood whispered, his voice filled with disbelief. The woman's face was serene, as if she had only just fallen asleep.

Gregg's mind raced as he recognized her from the Wondersun family portrait. It was Mary Wondersun, Raven's mother. Unlike Arthur, she appeared almost lifelike, as though the years had not touched her at all.

Before they could process what they were seeing, Sarah, Amy, and Jessica appeared in the doorway, leading the trembling Raven by the hand. The little girl looked even smaller in the dim light, her face pale and tear-streaked.

Gregg's eyes widened as he took in the sight of the girl. "Is that...?" he started to say, but Sarah quickly raised her hand, cutting him off. She nodded, confirming his suspicion.

Raven glanced around at the gathered group, her eyes brimming with tears. "I'm sorry," she whispered, her voice breaking. "I didn't want any of this. The mirror... it brings people here because it cares about me. That's why it gave me back my mom."

A tense silence enveloped the room as the group processed her words.

Sarah knelt beside Raven, her voice calm and reassuring. "Raven, what do you mean the mirror cares about you?" She asked, trying to sound calm, but her nerves showed.

"When I died, it pulled me in and brought me back. It promised me that nobody would get away with hiding dark secrets ever again. Like how daddy cheated on mommy."

Raven looked up with wide, frightened eyes. "At first, it was really nice to me," she said, her voice trembling. "It brought Mommy here to be with me, and I thought it was a place where we could stay together away from daddy. But after a while, I started feeling that something was wrong. I tried to leave, but the mirror wouldn't let me. It kept me here, and it made me see all these secrets."

Blackwood stepped forward, his expression serious. "Raven, the mirror isn't a friend. It's a evil entity," he explained. "It doesn't care about you. It's using you as a way to keep itself powerful. You were chosen because it feeds off the hidden, dark secrets of others. It's using you to spread its influence."

Raven's eyes widened, tears beginning to spill. "But why would it do that?" she asked, her voice breaking.

Blackwood's tone was firm but gentle. "By the look of it, it's driven by darkness and wants to cause pain. It uses people like you, people deeply affected by dark secrets to keep itself strong, feeding off the fear and sorrow it creates."

Sarah squeezed Raven's hand gently. "We're going to help you get out of here," she promised. "But we need you to be brave and help us break the mirror's hold."

Raven nodded, her small face determined. "I'll do my best," she said, her voice steady despite the tears. "I don't want to be here anymore."

Raven hesitated, her gaze drifting to her mother's preserved body. "But... what will happen to her?" she asked, pointing to her mothers body, her voice filled with fear.

Gregg stepped forward, his voice gentle but firm. "We don't know, Raven. But whatever happens, we'll be with you. You won't have to face it alone."

Suddenly, the whole room shook violently as it transitioned back into the black darkness. Mary Wondersun's body, now possessed by the entity, stood at the center. Raven screamed in terror as Sarah threw herself in front of Raven, shielding her from the malevolent force.

Blackwood, undeterred, quickly set up the ritual as the entity walked very slowly toward them. "All of you are never going to leave this place," it boasted.

Samuel placed a huge circle of salt, cinnamon, and pepper, with the dog collar bone in the middle. As the entity slowly walked over, it raised its hands as Sarah was suspended in the air. "I might not be able to pass that circle, but I can still do what I do best."

Gregg tried pulling Sarah down. "Snap out of it! We need—I need you," he exclaimed. However, the trance placed on Sarah was stronger this time. The entity laughed. "I can assure you, that's not working this time. Not now, not ever, are you taking her away from me," it said as it malevolently looked toward little Raven.

Sarah's mind was a whirlwind of guilt and despair. "I—I can't, Gregg. All I've ever done is fail. I'm a huge disappointment!" she cried out. "My mother died! And I wasn't there! Everything I do, I fuck up!"

Gregg looked up, his voice breaking as he shared a deeply buried memory. "I fucked up too. I got someone killed, someone close to me. My aunt Claire—I was a kid and threw a toy car in front of her, she tripped and—" Tears welled up in his eyes. "She impaled her neck. I killed her, and I'm always going to have to live with that. We're not human because we don't have faults; we're human because we do make mistakes, we fuck up sometimes, and that's okay."

The trance slowly started breaking. "How are you doing that?!" the entity screamed out.

"Fuck up, but don't push it down. Let it out. You are a good person. No matter how many times you've fucked up, you've made good for it," Gregg said, ending his speech. Sarah started to remember how happy she felt reuniting with Jenny, seeing her family, finally finding Jessica, and all the work she'd done as a detective. She fell to the ground as Blackwood began the Latin phrase.

With renewed focus, Blackwood started the ritual, chanting the long phrase again. However, once again, nothing happened. "Damn it!" he yelled out.

The realization hit Gregg. When he and Sarah were at the Wondersun estate in the real world, Arthur mentioned in his recordings that the ritual required a sacrifice. He turned to Sarah, reminding her of what Arthur said, and Sarah was the first to volunteer. "I'll do it," she stated.

"No, I'll do it," Gregg interjected. "Let me do this, Sarah. I didn't listen to you about the mirror thing. Let me have this."

Sarah stood her ground, shaking her head no as she stepped out of the ring, readying to sacrifice herself. Blackwood restarted the Latin phrase, and this time, it began to work. The dark area started to violently shake.

A light began to shine through the darkness, and an apparition of a mirror started to form. Gregg couldn't shake the thoughts of Sarah—their partnership, the bond they once shared, and the trust he had so carelessly broken. Every mistake he had made in the past weighed heavily on his mind, each one a reminder of how far he had strayed. In the end, he knew there was only one choice. If anyone had to go, it was him. As Blackwood finally finished the phrase, Gregg rushed and pushed Sarah back into the circle as a glass shard pierced his chest, blood violently pouring out.

"No!" Sarah cried out as the ritual reached its climax. The entity shrieked, its demonic howl piercing the air as its form disintegrated in the searing light. "Why the fuck would you do that?" she screamed, rushing to Gregg's side. He was struggling to breathe, his life slipping away as blood pooled around him.

Gregg looked up at Sarah, his vision blurring. "I'm... so sorry," he whispered, each word a struggle. "For everything—for breaking your trust... I thought... this was the only way to make it right." His voice faltered as he gasped for breath. "It's okay—it's gonna be... okay," he managed to say, a weak smile forming on his lips before the light in his eyes faded, and he passed away in her arms.

Panic surged through the group. They raced toward the mirror, desperate to escape. "Lawson! Come on!" Blackwood shouted as he bolted for the mirror, clutching Raven tightly.

Sarah hesitated, her eyes locked on Gregg's lifeless body. She couldn't just leave him here; it felt like a betrayal. With tears streaming down her face, she heaved Gregg's body onto her shoulder. It was heavy, almost unbearable, but she forced herself to move, her heart pounding as she ran toward the mirror.

Just as she reached the threshold, she cast one last glance back at the room, now eerily silent without the entity's presence. With a deep breath, she stepped through the mirror, carrying Gregg's lifeless body with her.

They all landed back in the real world, out of the mirror, back at the museum. They did it. They escaped the mirror: Sarah, Samuel, Danny, Jessica, Amy, and Raven. Not without a big loss, though.

Sarah cried over Gregg's lifeless body, holding his head close. Suddenly, the mirror shattered and faded into dust. In the next moment, at least three dozen small blue ball-like lights came out of the frame, circling the room. "What is it?" Jessica asked.

"Souls. Souls of the people it killed," Raven replied. The souls then formed a circle around Gregg, like they were giving their thanks and respects. They then flew out the window to finally rest in peace.

13 - Endings & Beginnings

We all carry pieces of our past that we'd rather forget—traumas and dark secrets that cling to us like shadows, shaping who we are in ways we might not even realize. These memories are like ghosts, haunting us no matter how fast or far we try to run. The truth is, you can't outrun your past. But what you can do is confront it, embrace it, and learn from it.

Trauma and dark secrets leave scars, both visible and invisible, etching themselves into our very being. These scars remind us of our vulnerabilities, of the moments when we felt shattered, lost, or afraid. It's easy to bury these memories, to lock them away in the deepest corners of our minds and pretend they never existed. But repression only tightens their grip on us, giving them more power over our lives.

Instead of running from the past, face it head-on. Acknowledge your pain, your regrets, your mistakes. Understand how these experiences have shaped the person you've become. This isn't about dwelling in sorrow or reopening old wounds—it's about accepting that these things happened and recognizing that they are an integral part of who you are today.

Embracing your past doesn't mean condoning it; it means finding the strength to move forward. Every experience, no matter how painful, carries with it a lesson. Perhaps it's a lesson in resilience, in how much you can endure and still rise. Maybe it's a lesson in empathy, teaching you how to connect with others who've suffered in similar ways. By learning from your past, you transform your pain into wisdom, turning scars into symbols of survival.

ONE WEEK LATER

A week passed, and life began to settle back into its usual rhythm, though it was forever altered by what had transpired. Sarah drove Jessica back to her grandmother's house, the journey silent but filled with unspoken relief. As they reached the small, familiar home, Jessica's grandmother rushed out, tears of joy streaming down her face as she gathered the girl into her arms, holding her as if she might disappear again at any moment.

Meanwhile, Danny and Amy returned to their own homes, trying to piece together some semblance of normalcy. They were safe now, but their eyes had been opened to the terrifying knowledge that the world was far more mysterious and dangerous than they had ever imagined. The comfort of their homes now felt fragile, the fear of the unknown lurking just beyond their doorsteps.

Sarah, however, found herself standing at the graveside of Gregg, her heart heavy with grief. The sky was overcast, mirroring the somber mood of those gathered. The pastor spoke words of comfort and peace, but they felt distant and hollow to Sarah. She watched as Gregg's mother collapsed in tears before his coffin, her sobs echoing the heartbreak that

Sarah felt deep within her own soul. His father stood beside her, a broken man, his eyes dull with sorrow.

They would never know the true story of Gregg's final moments—how he had bravely sacrificed himself to save others, how he had faced down a darkness that few could comprehend. To them, he was simply their son, a cop who lived and died in the line of duty. But to Sarah, and to those who were there with him in those final moments, Gregg was a hero, a man who had faced his own demons and found the courage to fight for others.

After the funeral, as the crowd slowly dispersed, Sarah lingered at the gravesite. She thought about everything that had happened, the horrors they had faced, and the courage Gregg had shown. A gentle breeze stirred the leaves, carrying with it a sense of finality, of something ending but also something being set free. She knelt down and placed a hand on the fresh earth covering Gregg's coffin.

"Thank you," she whispered, her voice catching in her throat. "I'm sorry it was you. But we're—*I'm* okay, thanks to you. I forgive you." She smiled as tears streamed down her eyes.

As she stood up, she felt a strange sense of peace. Gregg had found his redemption, and now it was time for her to find hers. The past would always be a part of her, but she knew now that it didn't have to define her. It could guide her, teach her, and help her become stronger.

Sarah walked away from the grave, leaving behind the weight of the past, but carrying with her the lessons it had taught her. Life would go on, but it would never be the same. And maybe, just maybe, that was okay.

As she walked toward the distance, she spotted Raven standing quietly, her small frame silhouetted against the fading light. Sarah quickened her pace, catching up to the girl. Raven turned to her, her eyes wide with curiosity and a hint of apprehension.

"So, what's next?" the nine-year-old asked, her voice carrying the innocence of a child but tinged with the wisdom of someone who had seen far too much.

Raven was a girl stuck in time, a relic of a bygone era. The last time she had been in the real world, it was 1956—a world of poodle skirts, Elvis Presley, and drive-in theaters. Now, in 2024, everything had changed, and Raven had a lot of catching up to do.

Sarah smiled softly, placing a reassuring hand on Raven's shoulder. "We take it one day at a time," she replied. "There's a whole new world out there waiting for you, Raven."

Raven looked up at Sarah, her eyes filled with a mix of hope and uncertainty. She had been trapped for so long, held in the grip of the mirror's dark power, that the prospect of a future—a real future—seemed almost too good to be true.

As Raven looked away, her gaze drifting toward the horizon, Sarah's thoughts turned inward. She hadn't ever imagined herself as a mother—hadn't thought she was capable of it, especially with all the demons she carried. The weight of her past, the guilt, and the regrets had convinced her that she was unfit to care for someone else, to be responsible for a child's well-being and happiness.

But as she watched Raven, this brave little girl who had been through so much, Sarah felt something shift inside her. Maybe she didn't have to be perfect. Maybe it wasn't about being free from demons but about facing them, together, with someone who understood what it meant to be haunted by the past.

Raven needed someone to guide her through the unfamiliar world she had been thrust into, and Sarah realized that, despite her doubts, she could be that person. They could help each other heal, one day at a time.

Sarah and Raven walked toward the car, its sleek modern design a marvel to the young girl who had only ever known the cars of the 1950s. As they reached the vehicle, Raven hesitated, her eyes wide with astonishment.

"I can't believe this is a car," Raven said, her voice filled with wonder. "It doesn't even look like one."

Sarah smiled, opening the door for her. "A lot has changed since you were last in the real world," she replied gently. "But don't worry, you'll get used to it."

They drove in comfortable silence, the weight of the recent past still heavy in the air but softened by the shared sense of relief. When they arrived at Sarah's apartment, Raven's eyes widened again at the sight of the four boxes stacked near the door.

"Are you moving?" Raven asked, her voice small.

Sarah nodded as they entered the apartment. "Yes, we're moving back to San Antonio. I want us to be closer to my family. I think it's important for both of us to have a fresh start."

Raven looked at the boxes, then back at Sarah, who knelt beside her. "When we get there, I'll buy you new clothes and toys, anything you need. You don't have to worry about anything, Raven. I'm here for you."

Tears welled up in Raven's eyes as she threw her arms around Sarah, hugging her tightly. "Thank you," she whispered. "For everything you've done and are doing."

As they pulled away from the embrace, Sarah's phone buzzed in her pocket. She pulled it out, seeing Blackwood's name on the screen. Answering it, she said, "Blackwood?"

"No need for formalities," Blackwood's voice came through with a light-hearted tone. "We destroyed a demonic entity together—call me Sam."

Sarah chuckled, "Alright, Sam. What's up?"

"I've been reflecting on everything we've been through. My father's legacy was built on power, control, and money, and I spent my life trying to undo what he stood for. I never thought I could truly change the impact of what he did. But after everything that's happened, I've realized I want to be a beacon of hope for those seeking peace and fighting against the darkness. You and Gregg—both of you helped me step out of my father's shadow."

His voice grew softer. "I'm deeply sorry about Gregg. If you ever need anything, remember you have a friend in Crestfall."

"Thank you, Sam," Sarah replied, her voice warm. "And you too, I'm here if you ever need anything."

She ended the call, a small smile playing on her lips as she reflected on the new beginnings that had emerged from the ending of the mirror's curse. Just then, a knock sounded at the door, interrupting her thoughts.

Sarah opened the door to find Dr. Joanna Christene, her therapist, standing there with a gentle smile. "Dr. Christene," Sarah greeted her. "Come in."

The therapist stepped inside, looking around the apartment. "I was a bit surprised when you asked to have our last session here, but I'm glad we could make it work."

They sat down, and Sarah gestured toward Raven, who was watching them with quiet curiosity. "I needed to be here to watch her," Sarah explained.

Raven offered a shy "Hi," and Dr. Christene smiled warmly at her. "Hi there," she replied, then looked back at Sarah. "Who is she?"

"She's family," Sarah answered simply, her voice filled with a new kind of certainty.

Dr. Christene nodded, understanding. "I heard about your mother's passing, Sarah. I'm so sorry."

"Thank you," Sarah said softly. "I've also reconnected with my sister, but losing my mom... it's been hard. And Gregg..."

Dr. Christene's expression softened even further. "I also heard about Mr. McAlaney. I'm truly sorry for your loss. I heard he died in the line of duty"

A faint smile crossed Sarah's face, and she took a deep breath. "Gregg, my mother, my father—they all lived amazing lives. They were incredible people. I've come to realize that when someone dies, you can either be a spectator of their legacy or an extension of it. I have to live by the example they set. I need to make them proud. I don't want to live life knowing that I'm doing wrong by them."

Dr. Christene looked at Sarah with admiration. "I couldn't have said it better myself. Our sessions are officially over, Sarah, but I want you to know how proud I am of you for embarking on this journey of healing."

"Thank you," Sarah replied, her voice filled with gratitude. "And speaking of new beginnings, Captain Wilson approved my transfer to the police station in San Antonio. I'll be closer to my family, to Jenny and Raven."

Dr. Christene smiled warmly. "That's wonderful news, Sarah. I'm confident that you're on the right path."

As the session came to an end and Joanna left, Sarah felt a sense of closure. She had finally let go of the heavy past that had weighed her down, but she knew she could never forget it. The memories of Gregg, her mom, and her dad were forever etched in her heart, shaping her into the person she had become. They were the reasons she was standing here today, ready to embrace a new chapter of her life.

She looked over at Raven, who was watching her with a mix of curiosity and determination. "Okay, let's get going," Sarah said, her voice filled with a new sense of purpose. "We've got to put these boxes in the car. The drive is three hours."

Raven nodded, stepping forward to help, though the box she picked up was light enough for her small frame. "Three hours is a long time," she said thoughtfully. "But I guess cars are faster now."

Sarah smiled at the comment, feeling a warmth in her chest. "They are. And we'll make it fun. We can talk, listen to music—maybe you'll even take a nap."

Raven smiled back as she began helping Sarah pick up the lighter boxes. They worked together, loading the car with the last of the boxes. Each one was a piece of Sarah's past, and as they packed them away, it felt like they were preparing to leave behind the old and step into the new. With the car loaded and the apartment empty, Sarah took one last look around before locking the door. This was the beginning of something different, something better, not just for her, but for Raven too.

As they climbed into the car and started their journey, Sarah glanced at Raven, who was gazing out the window with wide eyes, taking in the world that had changed so much since she had last seen it.

"Ready?" Sarah asked.

Raven nodded, her face full of wonder. "Ready."

THREE HOURS LATER

Sarah pulled the car up to the curb of Jenny's house, her heart pounding with a mix of excitement and nerves. The small, familiar house stood welcoming in the afternoon sun, and Jenny was already standing at the front door, her face lighting up as she saw the car pull in.

As soon as Sarah parked, she and Raven got out, and Sarah quickly rushed over to her sister, pulling her into a tight hug.

"You came back," Jenny said cheerfully, her voice filled with relief and happiness.

"Duh, sis," Sarah replied with a grin, pulling back slightly to look at Jenny. "I promised, didn't I?"

Jenny smiled, her eyes drifting to the little girl standing shyly by the car. "And this must be Raven?" she asked, her tone warm and welcoming.

Raven stepped forward, her hands clasped in front of her. "Hi," she said softly, her voice filled with a mix of curiosity and apprehension.

Jenny crouched down to Raven's level, giving her a reassuring smile. "Hi, Raven. I'm Jenny. I've heard a lot about you. And these two," she added, pointing to the two small girls peeking out from behind her legs, "are Jolie and Mary. Jolie's four, and Mary's three."

Raven's eyes widened slightly as she looked at the younger girls. "Mary was my mom's name," she said, her voice barely above a whisper.

Jenny's smile softened. "That's a lovely name. I bet your mom was wonderful."

Raven nodded, a small smile tugging at the corners of her mouth as she looked at the two little girls who were now smiling back at her.

Jolie and Mary, now feeling more confident, suddenly burst into giggles and rushed forward. "Do you want to play with us?" Jolie asked excitedly. "We're going to play freeze tag!"

Raven looked up at Sarah, her eyes full of hope and a silent question. Sarah smiled and nodded, giving her the permission she needed. "Go on, have fun," she said.

With that, Raven broke into a wide grin and took off after the two girls, her laughter joining theirs as they started playing in the yard.

Sarah and Jenny watched the girls for a moment, their hearts full as they saw Raven beginning to settle into her new life. Then, Jenny turned to Sarah, her expression serious but kind. "Thank you for coming back, Sarah," she said softly. "I know things haven't been easy, but I'm so glad you're here."

Sarah looked at her sister, her eyes filling with gratitude. "I should be thanking you, Jenny. For inviting me back into your life, even after everything I did."

Jenny shook her head, taking Sarah's hands in hers. "Hey, remember what Dad always said? 'We're sisters, we've gotta watch out for each other.' Nothing changes that, not ever."

Sarah smiled, her heart feeling lighter than it had in a long time.

The two sisters stood there for a moment, watching as Raven ran around with Jolie and Mary, her laughter echoing through the yard. It was a new beginning for all of them, a chance to heal and to move forward, together.

Author's Note

I understand how losing someone you care about can leave a deep void, a piece of your heart missing that lingers every day. I've experienced that pain myself; I lost my dad when I was just 13. Suddenly, I found myself navigating life alone, figuring out things a father is supposed to teach his son—how to shave, tie a tie, drive a car, and even prepare for that first job. Each of these milestones felt like another reminder of my loss.

Society often tells us that as men, we need to be strong and self-reliant, to handle everything on our own. While it's true that mentors and family members have their own lives and responsibilities, it doesn't mean you have to bear everything alone. There are people who care about you, who want to help you carry that burden. Whether it's friends, family, or someone you might not expect, accepting their support can make a world of difference. Remember, none of us are meant to go through life by ourselves.

Even in your deepest moments of pain, when the hole in your heart feels most profound, know that there are people ready to stand by you. They can't replace the one you've lost, but they can help you carry the weight of that loss. Sometimes, that support is what helps us find our way forward.

If you ever feel like you've let down those you've lost, if guilt or regret weighs heavily on you, it's important to find a way to let go of that burden. My uncle once told me, "When someone dies, you can either be a spectator of their legacy or an extension of it."

Even in the darkest times, remember you're not alone. Embracing help, continuing to grow, and choosing to honor the legacies of those we've lost are powerful steps. I believe in your ability to carry forward their legacy.

Dealing with trauma and dark secrets is a challenging journey, often easier said than done. The shadows of the past can seem overwhelming, but it's in these moments that our resilience shines brightest. Losing my dad young meant learning to navigate life and face challenges alone. It hasn't been easy, but each struggle has shaped me into who I am today.

Confronting the darkness within ourselves helps us gain strength. The lessons I've learned have been hard-won, teaching me perseverance, the importance of self-reliance, and the power of vulnerability. Struggling is part of the process, a sign that you are fighting for something better.

Sarah, who lost her father young, felt responsible and let that grief drive her into bad habits. She distanced herself from her family and regretfully chose not to reconnect. We all make mistakes—sometimes we say things we shouldn't, do things we regret, or fail to act when we wish we had.

For me, it was losing precious time with my dad because I was too engrossed in distractions like video games. It pains me to think that I didn't spend more time with him. Yet, I know he would have wanted me to continue, to support my family, and to be "the man of the house." That's his legacy—one of kindness, companionship, and love.

Though I made mistakes, I am committed to honoring his legacy, the legacy of kindness, companionship, and love.

Yours Sincerely,

Zayn Jamshaid

Did you love *Cracked Reflection*? Then you should read *Z-FORMULA* by Zayn Jamshaid!

About the Author

Zayn Jamshaid, a 16-year-old aspiring writer, faces numerous challenges as he strives for success. Zayn went through numerous challenges when he was young, which had an impact on his life, but he didn't allow that stop him from enjoying writing, spending time with family, reading comic books, playing video games, and practicing his spirituality.

Milton Keynes UK
Ingram Content Group UK Ltd.
UKHW030635071024
449371UK00001B/49